RIDE TO DAYLIGHT

RIDE TO DAYLIGHT

ALYSSA THIESSEN

Peasantry
PRESS

Ride to Daylight
Copyright© 2019 by Alyssa Thiessen

This title is also available as an e-book. Visit www.peasantrypress.com for information.

Information requests should be addressed to info@peasantrypress.com

Cover Design: Peasantry Press

A very special thanks to Winnipeg's *Bikes and Beyond*, whose advice, equipment, and group rides helped foster a love of the sport and a lasting passion for riding.

Library and Archives Canada Cataloguing in Publication

Title: Ride to daylight / Alyssa Thiessen.

Names: Thiessen, Alyssa, 1980- author.

Identifiers: Canadiana (print) 20190075937 | Canadiana (ebook) 20190075945 | ISBN 9781988276090

(softcover) | ISBN 9781988276106 (hardcover) | ISBN 9781988276113 (PDF)

Classification: LCC PS8639.H5365 R53 2019 | DDC jC813/.6—dc23

PEASANTRY PRESS
Winnipeg, Manitoba, Canada
www.peasantrypress.com

Dedicated to my bike-loving husband, Zig.
I'd face the end of the world with you
and your bikes any day.

CHAPTER 1

Tonight, she was thankful for the dark. She didn't used to be. When the lights first went out, darkness meant fear and chaos and violence. Now, it meant protection. If she couldn't see them, they couldn't see her, either. The streets were emptier on nights like these.

Crouching with her back against the cool brick of the apartment building, Robyn Kinley felt her way through the pile of debris trapped in the alleyway by the chain link fence. She'd crawled through the loose gating less than ten minutes ago. She didn't expect to find much. Nobody in their right mind would waste anything they were able to hold onto. Sometimes, though, she was lucky here.

Her fingers, stiff with cold, closed around what felt like a small tin can. She yanked it up. Too light. Empty. As an afterthought, she ran her fingers along the inside of the cylinder, checking if anything had been left. Slick. She let it fall as she continued rummaging. Several wrappers. A few empty cans. Paper. She fought back tears. Samantha and Meredith were waiting at home. They hadn't eaten in … how long had it been?

For Sam, at least two days. Longer for Meredith and herself. Kneeling, she swept her hand along the edge of the fence. The small stones and gravel scraped her palms, but there was nothing she could use.

A sudden breeze lifted the fog and the moonlight peered through the darkness, illuminating the street. Gunshots—two, in quick succession—shattered the quiet, and Robyn froze, her breath catching in her throat. It wasn't the sound itself that worried her but the proximity of it. The crunch of bicycle tires on pavement followed, and she stood, pulling her body in tight against the wall. Her apartment was only the next alley over, through the fence and down a block, but there was no way she would make it back before the rider reached her.

Robyn squinted through the dark into the far entranceway. A silhouetted rider swung around the corner, leaning forward on his bike, pedaling. He was going too fast for the loose grit lining the pavement, and the bike slid out, sending him and the bike skidding across the ground. The cyclist didn't move. Robyn waited for ensuing footsteps, but there were none. Not yet, anyway. She knew she didn't have long until they came looking for their target. Why wasn't he moving? She stepped out from the wall and knelt beside the man. As she rolled him over onto his back, he moaned softly.

He must have been hit. He was still alive, but just barely. He wore no colors. An Independent. He'd been counting on the cover of darkness, too.

She leaned in close to him. He blinked, his eyes glassy. His hand fluttered, moving to his stomach. Blood flowed through his fingers, seeping from a gaping hole in his abdomen. It soaked the fabric of his shirt and ran down onto the pavement. She felt her jeans dampening, and she touched his cheek. What could she do for him now? She glanced past him to his bike, less than a foot from where he lay. There were shouts from what couldn't be more than a block away.

They were almost here.

"I'm sorry," she whispered, realizing she had to leave him.

He grabbed her hand, shaking his head. Did he know what she was about to do? She gently slid her fingers from under his and stood. It was now or never.

Turning away from the dying man, she ran to his bike and lifted the handlebars from the ground. It was lighter than she'd expected, and she wheeled it to the fence. Peeling back the chain link, she grasped the seat post and guided the front of the bike through. The bike's metal frame scraped against the thin steel uprights of the fence. This was taking too long. She quickly pushed her way through the fence alongside the bike, biting back a cry when she caught her shoulder on the protruding chain link. Gritting her teeth, she turned and smoothed the fence back down. Her best shot was having them search the alleyway apartments surrounding the rider.

The voices were louder … closer. She swung her leg over the bike, putting her foot on the pedal and hoisting herself onto the seat. She hadn't been on a bike for over two years, but it felt like home. She stood as she pedaled, gripping the handlebars and focusing on the uneven terrain in front of her. The pavement was cracked and littered with debris and fine gravel. She knew the landscape, but she'd never ridden here. The darkness made it so much scarier.

She rounded the corner, pedaling down the main street. Shots rang out in the distance. If any Members saw her, she was as dead as the man she'd left behind.

I can do this. Back in California, she'd cycled competitively. In fact, at the time, she'd thought she'd been born to ride a bike. But she hadn't touched one since they'd crossed the Canadian border and got stuck in the small, miserable city of River Ridge.

An Electromagnetic Pulse, people had said. Whether from a solar flare or a terrorist attack was anyone's guess. She didn't care how it had happened, really. Maybe she had at the beginning, but now, all that mattered was surviving. When the blackout hit, it had taken a few days for everyone to accept that the electricity wasn't coming back on anytime soon, and a few weeks for them to realize help wasn't on its way either. Fires broke out and swept through the city. Sickness spread. People started dying. At the time, nobody knew how valuable a bike would be when it became the only means of transportation. They knew it now though. Now that it was too late. When the gangs had amalgamated to overrun the police force, they'd divided the city into territories and claimed everything, including the bikes. At least, the ones they could find.

Robyn swung into the next alley and hopped off the bike as she got to her building. She pulled up to the long, thin basement window.

"It's me!" she called down before yanking up the barred panel they used as covering and pushing the bike through. It clattered to the ground. She hopped in after it and pulled the window bars shut behind her. The room was black.

"Robyn?" Samantha whispered from the darkness, her voice thick with sleep. "What's happening? Are you okay?"

"Yeah. Shhhh."

"What was that?"

"Quiet."

"But …"

"Hush now, little one," Meredith's calming voice rasped from beside Sam. "Your sister will tell us all about it in the morning."

Sam released a heavy sigh. The bedsprings creaked as she settled back in to sleep.

Robyn turned to peer out the window. The street was still too dark for her to see anything. Her little sister's breathing slowed and deepened. Asleep already. Meredith was awake but silent. Despite the woman's seventy-two years, her eyesight was better than anyone's, and Robyn suspected she kept watch with her, from across the room.

Members from the Grims would be searching buildings for the bike tonight and in the light tomorrow.

I should have left it there. Should've just disappeared through the fence.

Members would have taken the bike and left everyone alone. But then what? Then they'd go back to starving to death. Now they had a real chance.

She peered out the window until her eyes grew heavy. The sky was lightening. Nobody was coming for them. She sat on the damp floor under the window. She'd have to lay low for a while until she could be sure they'd stopped looking for the bike. She pictured the dying man's face now, his eyes wide with horror as he realized she wasn't going to help him.

But what had he expected her to do? He was bleeding out and they were coming for him. It wasn't like she had medicine or training. Even if she had been able to pull him back with her, he'd never have survived. She would have risked her life for nothing. Taking the bike had been smart. It had been her only real choice. He would have done the same if their roles had been reversed. She used to believe people were generally good. Now she knew better.

* * *

"You got a bike?" Samantha's voice broke through the haze of sleep.

Robyn opened her eyes. She straightened her neck and struggled to her feet.

"Where'd you get it? Are you a Grim now?"

"Slow down." Robyn joined her beside the bike and they peered down at it. It was the first time she'd been able to see the thing clearly. She'd known the frame had to be carbon fiber as soon as she'd lifted it, but it was also in pretty great shape, considering what it had been through. Aside from the scratches she'd inflicted on it with the fence, the black and red paint was still decent. She righted it. It weighed next to nothing. The wheels were straight, the tires hard. It was slightly too big for her, but she'd manage. "It's perfect," she whispered.

"Where did you get it?" Sam asked again, her brown eyes huge. She wasn't looking at the bike anymore, but up at Robyn, waiting. A bike like this wasn't something anybody just picked up.

"I found it," Robyn answered quietly, "but the Grims are looking for it, so we need to be careful."

Sam's small hand clutched hers. "What will you do with it?"

"Ride. As an Independent."

Robyn waited for her sister to protest. She just whispered, "Don't die, okay, Robyn?"

"Promise." It was an empty promise, like most of the ones she made these days. Like her promise to bring them something to eat. Sam didn't mind empty promises, though. At six, she knew their reality.

"So what now?" Meredith asked, rising.

"Now I guess I'll hide the bike and go out again. Try to find us something to eat. Maybe I'll hit the exchange region," Robyn said.

"The bike would be worth something," Meredith said. "If you bartered it, you could get—"

"I could get killed. This bike is only any good to us if I'm riding it."

Meredith frowned but said nothing more. Robyn didn't want to argue. Meredith had no idea what things were really like out there. She kept Sam inside with her like Robyn asked, but she didn't understand. She didn't' realize those animals didn't care about your age, your faith, your looks. Just about ease of prey. Meredith couldn't know how much they all risked every time Robyn gave into Sam's pleading for sunshine and led them onto the roof.

Samantha grabbed Robyn's empty backpack. Meredith rose and pushed the small bed across the floor, away from the sliding closet door. She pulled it open, revealing the boxes stacked to the ceiling inside. Robyn helped her move the boxes aside, opening the makeshift entrance into the empty adjoining room. Robyn wheeled the bike through.

Meredith and Robyn had smashed their way through the wall when they first found this place. The apartment building had been largely destroyed in the fires, but the basement walls were mostly intact. There wasn't a lot of competition for them either because lower rooms like these were where the rats congregated, not to mention the constant damp and mildew. But it was safer than out there, and the fact there were so many suites empty meant they were able to set up this panic room. It was also their emergency exit, since it's door opened into a different hallway than their room did.

With the bike tucked away, Robyn replaced the boxes, slid the closet door closed, and helped Meredith move the bed back to its original position.

She took the backpack from her sister and slung it over one shoulder. She remembered when it actually contained goods to trade. Now it was merely for show.

"Take care of each other," she said as she turned to the window. It was always the last thing she told them before leaving, and the sentence hardly even meant anything anymore. But if she didn't make it back home, Robyn wanted it to be the one thing they remembered.

Take care of each other. Her mother's final words echoed in Robyn's ears. The nightmares had faded by now, but sometimes she still saw that group of red bandanas—*Grims*—in her mind, surrounding her parents a few feet from where she and Sam had hidden under their red, immobile Suburban two years ago.

"Look at me," Robyn had whispered, turning her head towards her sister.

Sam, then four, instantly obeyed. The two stayed with eyes locked on one another while their parents were murdered. Sam hadn't even cried. Not during the attack, not while the gang pillaged what was left of their belongings. So much for escaping the city on foot.

And that was before the gangs had organized. Now, with their own names and territories, gangs cooperated to keep the people in line. A person could get past their patrols if they really wanted— get out, maybe—but then what? Here, at least, they were relatively safe. Shelter. Some semblance of order. She stayed for Sam.

But I'll die before I ever turn to those animals for help, Robyn thought.

Robyn grabbed her Dodgers cap from the windowsill—one

of the few things she'd hung on to from home, and pulled it on, shading her eyes. The alleyway was clear. Without a backwards glance, Robyn pushed open the window and crawled out onto the pavement. She hurried along the brick wall and then crossed the street. She kept her chin up and her strides long; she avoided eye contact with the few people she passed. She tried to imagine she was armed. Not that it would guarantee her safety, but it would help. She kept her long hair tied back anytime she went out. Poker straight and a natural, deep auburn, it used to be one of her favorite features. Now, it made her a target.

She should have chopped it all off by now. The less feminine she looked, the better, although she didn't feel particularly feminine anyway, these days. She'd lost so much weight that, with her five-one frame, she felt more like a child than an eighteen-year-old woman. She shook her head at herself. *The world's gone insane, but at least I have my hair.*

Truth was, Sam wanted her to keep it long. It reminded her of Mom. Robyn couldn't do much for Sam, but she could keep her hair.

As she approached the Exchange, she took a deep breath. *Nobody can hear your heart pounding.*

The Exchange was the closest thing they had to a civilized market now but, even there, even under the watch of the Grims, people were mugged—and worse. The trick to surviving was to be invisible. Invisible, but not afraid. Somehow, the Grims could smell fear.

Robyn glanced around as she entered the square, looking for the ones who might have food. Food was much scarcer now. People were more likely to have candles, clothing.

There were only a few people standing around. Slim pickings. Members from the Grims were there too, as usual, mostly in the street entrances. They were lightly dressed, even though the November weather had begun to cool, with their signature red rags around their heads and necks, and their sawed-off shotguns slung carelessly over their shoulders. Some would have other pieces tucked into their waistbands, or holstered, or strapped to their legs. Their bikes were propped up together against one of the nearby walls. They didn't even pretend they were there to keep order; they were waiting for someone to make a trade, and then they'd take a cut.

Animals.

When the lights went out, who would have thought the ones who would step in and take control would be the gangs?

She casually leaned against the wall. Last time, she'd grabbed a sack from someone distracted by a conversation and put it inside her own. She'd walked away with it before they'd even realized it was missing. Today, though, everyone seemed to be on their guard.

"What're you trading?" A gruff voice startled her and she straightened up quickly.

"You first." She glanced at the speaker. His unkempt, graying beard would have been frightening before. Now, it was commonplace. Most men didn't bother to shave anymore. Besides, a good razor was hard to come by. And worthless in the marketplace, as she'd discovered months ago when she'd broken down and tried to trade hers.

"Medicine."

She raised her eyes. "What kind?"

"Inhalers. Salbutamol."

Her eyebrows shot up. Impossible. Not that she needed it, but stuff like that barely surfaced on the market. "Where'd you get it?"

He lowered his voice, leaning in close. "Used to work at

Grace Hospital. A few days after the blackout, when everything was goin' nuts, I grabbed our entire emergency stock. My wife had asthma since she was little."

"Why are you trading it now?"

"She won't be needing it anymore." His voice was flat. "What can you give me for it?"

Robyn's face flushed. She wished she'd told him she didn't need it in the first place.

Before she could reply, a low, nasally voice broke in from her right. "I have canned food here. You can have three tins for your supply." It had to be a Member. There was no way anyone else would offer so low.

"You kidding?" The man pulled his bag in close to his chest. "This stuff is worth—"

"It's worth what I say it's worth. Just reduced my offer to two." As he spoke, the Member slid his hand around Robyn's waist. Her skin crawled as she glanced up at his face. A ruddy complexion, with little facial hair beyond a thin blond mustache, made him seem even younger than she was. She fought the urge to shove him. He wouldn't think twice about killing her.

Run. She wished she could transfer her thoughts to the guy with the medicine. *Just run and give me a break.* He wasn't moving, though. He was no more a fool than she was, and her heart sank as he began to loosen his hold on the bag.

"Jared!" a frantic voice yelled from across the square, and the three of them looked up. Black smoke filled the air, wafting up from the side of the adjacent building. "Jared! Someone help! Quick!"

The boy pulled his arm away from Robyn and sprinted across the square to the other Members. The Grims there were beating the flames down with their jackets. If unchecked, the fire would take out the entire neighborhood. They needed to stop it if they were going to keep their territory intact. The medicine man had already taken the opportunity to disappear.

Robyn darted across the street to the fire. She could see that the Members had pulled off their jackets and thrown down their packs. As if they were untouchable. Robyn grabbed the pack with the cans and swept up the other two closest to it, then ran. She didn't look back or slow down until she rounded the corner to her own alleyway. As she neared her window, she glanced over her shoulder. Black smoke billowed up in the distance, but the street was clear. In one quick, fluid motion, she pulled open her window and slid inside.

Breathing heavily, she dropped the bags on the floor, then bent and rested her hands on her thighs.

"You okay?" Sam was at Robyn's side.

"Fine in a minute."

"What did you find?" Meredith asked. *Find.* That was a funny way of putting it. "And do I smell smoke?"

"There was a fire in the marketplace. I think it's far enough away that we'll be okay, but we'll watch for it. Let's be ready to move if we have to."

"And the packs?" she asked.

Robyn bent down and picked up the one with the cans, tossing it at Meredith. She caught it and her eyes widened.

"Food, Meredith. We have food."

Sam picked up one of the other bags on the floor and pulled it open. "This one has food in it too, Robyn. Look." She held it open. Carrots. The second bag was full of carrots. She pulled one out and handed it to her older sister. They hadn't seen fresh produce for nearly a year. Meredith put down the bag she was holding and came to join them. She gasped as she bit into it.

"They have vegetables!" Robyn's anger rose again. The Members were growing food now. Growing it! And still people were starving to death. She handed the bag to Sam, and her little sister reached in again for more. Robyn opened the third pack: shotgun shells, switchblades, and lighters. She pulled out one of the knives and flicked it open. The long, thin, silver blade caught the light from the window. It was still sharp. She snapped it closed and shoved it into her pocket. What was she supposed to do with the rest of this stuff? Trade it, she guessed, although trading their own supplies back to the Members probably wasn't the most intelligent idea she'd come up with, and that was pretty much her only market. Well, that and the Independents. But business with an Independent was a risk itself.

A knock rattled the window. The three of them froze. Dark blue jeans with black sneakers stood at the opening and mildly kicked again at the bars. The figure bent down to peer in at them; unfamiliar dark blue eyes—almost charcoal—gazed their way. The young man's face was stubbled, and his brows were drawn in a slight frown. He wore a red rag around his neck.

"Hope you're not armed, because I'm coming in," he said.

CHAPTER 2

"Oh, no, you're not," Robyn moved to stand in front of Meredith and Sam. In the year they'd lived here, nobody had bothered them. Nobody had come to the window. Nobody had shown any interest in them at all. She must have been followed. She'd led him right to them. How could she have been so careless?

"Listen, unless you want me to report back to my crew about the bike you took last night and the bags you stole this morning"—he pointed a dull black pistol through the window in their direction—"or maybe just shoot you where you stand, you'll courteously step back from the window with your hands raised."

"Robyn?" Sam looked up at her, already raising her little fingers in the air.

They were trapped. If they didn't do what he wanted, there was nothing stopping him from shooting them. But if they did…

Meredith took a step back to stand beside Sam, her hands raised high in the air. What Robyn would have given for a window lock.

"Please don't hurt them," Robyn said finally, dropping the ammo bag and lifting her arms. "I took the bike and the bags.

They had nothing to do with anything." Maybe she could rush him when he came inside. He pulled open the window with the same hand that held the gun and climbed down, landing sharply on one leg. Wincing, he leaned against the wall and fixed the gun on them again. He had to be a few years older than she was—tops—and his face was carefully stoic. His shaggy, dishwater-blond hair hung down into his eyes.

"I'm not planning to hurt anyone," he said calmly. "I just thought we could help each other." He lowered his gun and took his gloved finger from the trigger. Very slowly, he slid the gun into the waistband of his jeans. "And you're welcome for the fire, by the way."

The fire? "You expect me to believe that was you?"

He shrugged. "Don't care. Believe it or not, I'm not really looking to build a lasting friendship here."

"What are you looking for?"

"Thought we could come to an … arrangement."

Robyn instinctively stepped backwards, shuddering. She'd managed to make it this far without selling herself. Her expression must have made her thoughts obvious because he laughed. The sound was hollow and too loud in the small space.

His smile faded. "Don't flatter yourself. I'm not looking for that kind of arrangement."

"Then what?"

"You have a bike. I know an Independent. He could show you some stuff, like how to not get caught, the routes you can trust, et cetera. And I know the Grims' delivery schedule." He pushed himself up off the wall. "If it's all the same to you, ladies, I'm going to sit down now." He limped past them towards the white, rectangular table in the center of what would have once been the kitchen.

Robyn ran through escape possibilities. Something was clearly wrong with his leg. If she could throw him off balance, or maybe …

"Listen, hear me out before you and the family make a break for it," he said without turning. "Do you really think you'd be able to survive as an Independent on your own? You against the Grims and their allies in this city? I'm your best shot."

"Why? Why would you help me?"

He held up his left hand. The thin black leather covering the fingers curved inwards; his hand twisted and clenched at an unnatural angle. "The Grims aren't exactly a charity. I can't ride a bike anymore. No good in a foot race. But I know my blood type—O Neg—so they think they can to use me for blood if they need to. And I'm good for intel." He tapped his head. "As close to a photographic memory as they've seen. I know this city blindfolded. They pay me for services rendered but, between jobs, I'm on my own. And it's hungry on my own."

Robyn steeled herself against the rising pity at his twisted, useless hand and the painful limp. Regardless of where he was now, he was still one of the Grims. He wore their colors around his neck. He fed them information. He promised them *blood*. But what choice did she really have?

"What would your help mean?" she finally asked.

"A partnership. I supply you with the information you need to stay alive and turn a profit, and we split your take two ways."

"There are four of us."

He looked at her. "I can count. We split it in half, or I walk out of here, loyal to the Grims. And they come back for the bike."

No, she wasn't sorry for him. He was an animal like the rest. Just a smarter one.

"Fine," she said. "You have a deal. Now get out."

"I'll give the Independent your address or, better yet, I'll bring him here myself. Don't go anywhere. I don't want to have to look for you." He stood and limped over to them. Leaning down, he pulled a carrot from the open produce bag at their feet. He grinned. "They're gonna be mad about this one." He bit into the carrot and chewed slowly. "Don't worry, though. Your secret's safe with me." He winked, and then, with his good arm, hoisted himself up through the window and crawled out into the night.

As soon as he was gone, Meredith sprung to life. "Quickly now." She pushed the bed away from the closet entrance. "Grab the food. We can go through the apartment building and exit out the back. There may still be some empty suites in the basement rooms over on Smith. Didn't you say some of the buildings were still standing?"

"We're leaving?" Sam asked quietly.

"Yes," Meredith replied.

At the same time, Robyn said, "No."

"No?" Meredith's voice cracked. "Did you just say no?"

"I don't know how he found us in the first place. But, if he found us once, who's to say he can't find us again? You heard him. I can't risk it."

"So, what? You're planning to trust him? Robyn, we have food now, and—"

"And what? What about when it runs out?" Robyn asked, nauseous. "He's right. I can't do it alone. I hate him—trust me, I do, Meri—but he's the only chance we have right now."

"What if he sends them back here?"

She chewed her lip. Meredith had a point. Robyn had already thought of the solution, although she knew Sam wasn't going to like it. "You and Sam move to the panic room. Here."

She swept the blankets off the bed, balling them up. She handed them to Meredith. "It's not the greatest, but it will do for now." She handed Sam the two bags with the food. "Bring these with you. If they come back, they'll only find me. I'll tell them the two of you are gone. You can get out the other hallway."

"Robyn, don't be foolish."

"I won't go," Sam clenched her jaw, her round face set in a determined expression. She stepped away from the closet door. "You can't make me. If you think he's going to help us, then we don't need to hide. If you think he's lying, then I'm not going to just leave you here."

"Sam ..."

"I mean it!" She crossed her arms and backed against the farthest wall. Sam had been four when the power went out, and one of the most docile kids Robyn had ever known—so unlike herself at that age. Now, at six, Sam was a carbon copy of her big sister, from her brown eyes and thick, reddish straight hair to her stubborn determination. Usually, it came in handy. The world was a different place than it had been. But at times like this, Sam was frustrating and dangerous.

"I only *think* he's telling the truth." Robyn gritted her teeth, trying to be patient. "But I can't risk you and Meredith if I'm wrong."

"Then you can't risk *yourself* either."

"Sam, listen to me." Robyn stepped towards her, and Sam's eyes narrowed.

"I'll scream. I mean it. You can't hide us if I'm screaming."

Robyn sighed, surrendering. "Then we all leave. Now."

Meredith slid open the closet door. "Good. We'll exit through the panic room then. Just in case." She pushed the stack of boxes from their secret entranceway.

"But what about what you said, Robyn?" Sam's voice quieted. "That it's our best shot—"

"Forget what I said. I'm not willing to gamble with your lives." Robyn gestured with her head towards the room. "Let's go, then."

"You really think it's not a trick?"

"I think it's not. But I'm not always right, am I?"

"But you are, most of the time." Sam's swiped at a tear, and Robyn knew she'd won. "If we hide, promise you'll shout if you're in trouble."

"Promise." Again, it wasn't one she intended to keep, but it didn't matter. It was enough.

Sam threw herself against Meredith and hugged her tightly around the waist.

"Shhh," Meredith whispered against Sam's hair, wrapping her arms around her.

Robyn knew Meri still didn't like it, but Sam would be safe. As Meredith led Sam through the door, Robyn followed, bringing them the blankets and backpack. There was a small, metal bed frame in the room from the previous tenants, and she laid the blankets on it in a heap. She set the food on the floor and took out a tin of tuna for herself.

Leaning in towards Meredith, she whispered, "Listen for trouble. If there's anything that doesn't sound right, get out. Take everything and go."

Sam still wasn't looking at her, but Robyn squeezed her shoulder before going back through the closet entranceway.

She stacked the boxes again, slid the closet door closed, and pulled the bed back into place. Sitting on the bare mattress, she leaned her back against the wall beside the closet door. They were often quiet in here together, but it felt deathly silent without the two of them. She peeled back the tabbed lid on the can. The smell of fish filled the small space. In the past, she hated stuff like this. Fish was bad enough, but *canned* fish? No way. Now, though, canned anything was all most people had left. She scooped out the soft mess with her fingers. What would people do when this stuff started to go bad? Two years was pushing it. But in five years? Ten? Would everyone in River Ridge starve to death?

She thought about the carrots. Somewhere in the city, people were growing things again. She wished she'd brought some of that fresh produce in here with her. She guessed she could go back in and get something, but she didn't know how long it would be until she had company, and she couldn't risk timing it wrong and giving the other two away.

* * *

Darkness descended, and the city of River Ridge became alive with shadows. Robyn considered lighting a candle. Would Sam and Meredith, sitting on the empty bed frame, be talking quietly or just listening? It was surprising how quickly they had become used to the long stretches between daytime activities, with nothing but conversation or their own thoughts to fill the time. Conversation, at this point, was an impossibility. But her thoughts weren't particularly good company either.

Robyn crossed the room and stood on her tiptoes to stare out the window. The moon was high and bright enough to dimly light the streets. The Independents would be more active now. Members from all the territories mostly traveled during the day. It was safer during daylight hours as long as everyone stayed in their own territories. Night was when the Independents rode. Under the cover of darkness, they worked the routes most amicable to their softer way of doing things. Independents charged less to carry messages and goods than the Members did, and they weren't as likely to take what you offered as payment and not finish the job.

She'd dealt with an Independent before, when she still had goods to trade. He'd been old for a rider; close to forty, she'd guessed. He had reminded her of her own father. She'd asked him to find blankets for Sam and her, and he'd brought her one. She'd traded the owner two boxes of matches and paid the rider two more. By then, she had learned to light her own fire with flint and steel.

It had been a good trade for everyone. Afterwards, though, she had thought about the person who had traded blankets for matches. How long would the matches have lasted?

She hadn't seen the Independent again, although he had promised to come back. Later, she was relieved. She hated dealing with Grims and avoided it when she could. But if they had caught her doing business with an Independent, she'd have had worse things to worry about than overpaying.

She gazed into the street, barely blinking. It was dark, even with the moonlight filtering down. It would be difficult to see them coming. Farther down the alley, she thought she saw something move on the other side of the street—just outside of her line of sight—then dart across to her building. She couldn't see them now; they were up against her wall. She strained to listen. What if he'd sold her out? Should she hide? Her apartment was dark enough that, maybe, by the time they got in and lit it up, she would be able to get around them and out. The idea was impossible, of course. She could never leave her sister behind, hidden or not. She took a step back. If the Grims were coming, she would go down fighting before they had a chance to get anything from her.

Footsteps approached now, but not many. It was no raid.

"You still in there?" the masculine voice from earlier called down to her. "I brought the Independent."

She took another step back.

One shadowed figure dropped down into the room, almost entirely invisible in the darkness. "Pass me your bike, Trev." It was the Grim.

She heard a grunt, and then the moonlight completely disappeared as a large bike was handed down through the long window. There was a slight noise as the Grim leaned the bike, she assumed, against the wall.

The second figure lowered himself in. "Where are you?"

Robyn heard a metallic clink as what sounded like a lighter case opened and then the scritch of the flint wheel. The Grim held it out in front of him. She could just barely see his face, his high cheekbones giving him a gaunt, almost ghost-like appearance.

"Could we get a little light in here? We weren't followed," he said.

Fingers trembling, she turned from his light and groped for the table. She moved past it to the small, yellowed cabinet she knew was along the wall. Reaching into the thin wooden drawer, she pulled out one of the votive candles she had left. She'd heard that people had started making them again so she knew she could probably get another if needed.

"Here," she said. She followed his light back to him. She touched the gloved hand that held the lighter—steadied it— as she guided the candle to the flame with her other hand. For some reason, the simple contact felt more intimate in the dark. One would think that, with so little light, people would touch more, but the opposite was true. People couldn't trust what they couldn't see.

The flame flickered for a moment and then grew bright, softly lighting the small room.

"You couldn't find anything to use for window coverings?" the Independent asked, drawing their attention to him.

"Not starving was more of a priority," Robyn said, finally turning her attention away from the Grim. The Independent was a few inches shorter, although both men had the lean, long frame of cyclists. His features were softer though, and his eyes were deeply set, although she couldn't make out their color in the candlelight.

He smiled. "Trevor West," he said. "I've been an Independent now since right after the fires, after most of the bikes were gone— or taken—by Members."

"So, how do you know him?" she asked, inclining her head towards the Grim.

"I've known Coop since we were eight years old," he said. "We practically grew up together."

"Coop?" she said.

"Nate Cooper. Gone by 'Coop' for as long as I can remember."

"Oh," she said. *Nate Cooper.* It was strange to think of the Grim having a name, growing up somewhere before any of this, actually having a history like a normal human being.

"How come Nate lucked out with membership and you didn't?" Robyn asked.

"I was in the Grims before the blackout," Nate said. "Joined when I was fourteen."

"So where's this bike?" Trevor asked.

Robyn was momentarily relieved. The less she knew about Nate's personal life, the better.

The bike! *Stupid, stupid, stupid!* She'd hidden Meredith and

Sam in the same room as the bike. She should have known these two would want to see it.

"Coop wants me to show you some things. Figured we might as well start tonight," Trevor said, when she didn't move to retrieve the bike.

"I'm not going tonight." When Nate raised his brows, she crossed her arms. "You know they'll be watching for riders." She pictured the man she'd taken the bike from, the look in his eyes as she pulled it away from him, as he realized he was dying. He'd probably thought it was as good a night as any, too. "It's too soon still. Give it a few days."

"What, and give you time to skip out on me?" Nate asked.

"Where would I go?" She could think of a dozen places she scoped out that she could move to, but nowhere Nate or the Grims wouldn't eventually find her in. They were pretty adept at hunting people they wanted caught.

"She's right about waiting." Trevor laid his hand on Nate's shoulder. "There's going to be a lot of heat right now. The other Independents are talking about Mike. Everyone knows the Grims killed him and that they're looking for his bike. Most Independents are laying low, too."

"Fine. Two days," Nate said. "I know the guys. They'll get bored and the heat will ease off."

"Three," Robyn said. He wasn't going to set the terms this time.

Nate shrugged.

"Nice meeting you," Trevor said, his voice sounding a little strained.

"Can't say I feel the same." She didn't have anything against Trevor. He wasn't a Grim. But he *was* helping Nate force her to work for him.

Trevor turned and pulled himself up through the window. He reached down for his bike, which Nate hefted up with his good arm. Trevor pulled it through. Nate turned as if to go, but, at the last minute, hesitated. His eyes swept the room once more. He half-smiled as he leaned in towards her.

"Let me guess. Your bike is with the kid and old lady?" He let his gaze drift towards the closet and then back to her.

She didn't reply, and he laughed, then turned back towards the window. His threat wasn't lost on her. He knew they were still here; he was making sure she knew he knew.

"Just get out," Robyn said.

Nate pulled himself up with his good arm and disappeared through the window. She waited. There was no way Nate would let her have the last word. Sure enough, after a beat, his head appeared at the window again. "See you in two."

CHAPTER 3

"You going to do a run anyway?" Nate asked, as he and Trevor stood in the dark against the building just outside the girl's apartment.

"Think so. A short one."

"Be careful." Nate tried to keep his voice even. Every time Trevor went, there was a good chance he'd be caught. If he were caught, Nate knew, the Grims would make sure Trevor served as a public—and gruesome—example of the consequences of defying the Grims and its Members. Despite the risks, though, Nate couldn't blame him. Given half a chance to ride again, he'd risk everything. After the accident, the Grims had repossessed his bike, not that he could ride it anymore anyway. But at least they hadn't completely disowned him.

"You be careful, too," Trevor said, doing nothing to mask the emotion in his own voice.

"I'm a Member. They'd have no reason not to trust me."

"Be careful anyway, Coop." Trevor mounted his bike and, with a quick wave, started out again, disappearing into the night.

Nate wondered what it would have been like if he'd never joined the Grims. He looked at his deformed hand. He wouldn't have had the injury. As quickly as the thought struck him, he reminded himself of the truth: if the Grims hadn't found him, he wouldn't have had the injury because there was no way he would have lived to see the Blackout. They'd saved him. They were his family. A dysfunctional one, considering the fact he was using some girl they were looking to kill—as an Independent— to make money for himself and keep it from the Grims, but what family wasn't a little dysfunctional? Besides, if they'd taught him one thing, it was that you had to look after yourself.

He started down the street, ignoring the usual pain that shot through his thigh every time his heel made contact with the ground. He wouldn't sleep, as usual. The cold made it worse.

He tried to pick up the pace. He wanted to be at home, if any Members stopped by. They usually didn't at night, but sometimes they did. And being at home was a good alibi. They'd expect him to be there if someone got cut. They might need his blood, and that was worth something.

It was a fairly short walk from her place to his, which was why he'd found her in the first place. She'd been digging around in the debris outside his apartment in the middle of the night as if she thought she were invisible. It had been dark, but he'd heard her clearly enough, and he knew exactly who it was—the same little fool he'd seen out there several nights earlier and a few weeks before that. The same girl he'd seen more than once in the market. She was interesting looking, with her long, dark brown-red hair that seemed to always be falling into her eyes when it wasn't tied back and covered with that stupid ball cap. Anyone who'd let themselves be recognized like that deserved whatever they got. When the sky cleared and she straightened, he'd considered taking her. She was skinny, like most of them these days, but her small, lithe body was definitely intriguing.

He'd bet, from her desperate scavenging, that she'd be willing to trade herself for some of the food he'd stored up. And if not, it wasn't like she could put up much of a fight anyway, even with his bad leg. He'd pushed the thought away. He'd never forced himself on anyone, although he'd used his position in the crew as leverage to get what he wanted.

After she'd taken the bike and pushed her way back through the gate, he'd considered telling the Grims what he saw. When his crew had come to his door, he'd considered it again. But what did he really know, anyway? And how much more would they reward him if he found her himself?

And now you have found her, he reminded himself. So why hadn't he turned her in?

At his apartment, he leaned on the railing and limped up the steps. Before he got to the door, he turned at the slow whir of tires on the pavement behind him. He could just make out the figures of two Members approaching slowly down the quiet street. They talked as they patrolled, their hushed voices barely carrying to where he stood. He'd never imagined *bicycles* would be a status symbol. He'd had his Yamaha picked out for years, the motorbike he'd ride with the Grims when he got his license. Now those bikes were scrap metal. He shook his head. *Bicycles.* Not that he could ride one of those anymore either.

He turned back to the door, unlocked it, and went inside. He pushed it closed and turned the deadbolt. He knew why he hadn't turned her in. Captured, the Grims would enjoy a few hours of entertainment before they eventually killed her. But if she worked for him, as an Independent for now—maybe as something more lucrative in the future—there would be no limit to his profits. She was more useful alive and in his possession.

Avoiding the small coffee table in the middle of the room,

Nate limped through the black room towards his bedroom door. The apartment was spacious, comparatively. Two bedrooms were hard to come by since the fires, and they were reserved only for Members. He'd almost lost his place after the accident. When he couldn't ride, after they'd claimed his bike, one of the guys had suggested to the Grims he be forced to surrender the colors. There'd been a vote. It had been a narrow win in his favor, but a win was a win.

Sitting heavily on his bed, he listened to the night. Every now and then, the silence was broken by shouts or screams or gunshots. He'd grown up in this city; it had never really been a safe place to live, not for him. Of course, it was worse now. He pulled out his pistol and laid it on the stand by the bed.

He leaned his back against the smooth, cool wall. Flexing his bad foot, he massaged his leg, willing the blood to return. This wasn't the way it was supposed to be. He was supposed to be out there patrolling with his crew, ruling the pathetic, helpless city with them.

Now who's helpless?

Tired, he closed his eyes. He didn't mind the dark. The damaged muscles in his calf were still so tight that lying down was out of the question.

His eyes flew open at frantic banging on his door. It had to be the Grims. The thick red X on his door, identifying him as a Member, would have discouraged anyone else from coming near his place.

"Coming!" he called as the rattling increased. "Just hang on!" He didn't want them to break it down before he reached it, but all the walking he'd done earlier was catching up with him and slowing him down.

"Hurry up, Coop." Jared Ward's panicked voice carried

through the door.

Nate quickly turned the lock and yanked the door open. Jared rushed in first, heading directly for the cupboard where they kept the suture kit. Nate stood back as Jared's patrol partner, Rob, followed, completely supporting the weight of their third, whose arm was limply slung around Rob's shoulder.

"That Owen? What happened?" Nate turned towards the counters and reached for his lighter. He methodically lit the candles that lined the countertops and then carried one of the largest ones over to the coffee table.

"Owen caught an Independent trying to do a delivery on Ryerson. They got into it, and the guy stuck him in the stomach. It's deep. He's bleeding pretty bad."

"Did you see what he looked like?" Nate asked as he helped Jared spread out a large white sheet on the floor, where they'd work on Owen. They tried to keep it as sterile as possible. A clean sheet would keep out dirt and curb the risk of infection but, in these conditions, there wasn't much else they could do.

"Yeah. Rob went after him. He's done."

Done, Nate thought. *They killed him.*

"Some short freckled kid."

Nate kept his face blank. It wasn't Trevor. "Did you send for a doc?"

"No time. We'll go after." Jared's lighter flashed, then brightened as he sterilized the needle. As Jared began his work, Owen, barely conscious before, screamed before falling silent. He'd passed out.

Nate knew that, any day now, they could collect on his promise of blood. He'd seen others donate. Some of the docs had salvaged field transfusion kits from the hospitals, with proper syringes and anticoagulants to keep the blood from clotting during the transfusion. It wasn't great, but a few of those transfusions worked out okay. Fatalities were a given—more fatalities than not— but it was still better than the alternative. The docs, without the right supplies, used direct donation, artery to vein—primitive and messy and damaging. The donor usually didn't make it. The recipient's survival was a crapshoot at best.

Of all the ways to die around here, giving blood to Owen was the least appealing. Owen had voted against keeping Nate in the Grims. If he had his way, Owen would feel every stitch. And better than that, he'd die before Nate had to share a drop.

Not that Nate was scared of death. He never had been, even before. When he'd joined the Grims before the blackout, he'd known a lot of the Members never made it to their eighteenth birthday. In the first year as a Member, he'd lost one of his friends to a drive-by and another to an overdose.

After the blackouts and the fires, after Marshall Ward had united the city gangs, that lack of fear had been what secured him a position working alongside Marshall's son, Jared. And after the accident, when he faced the vote without begging or so much as flinching, his courage was what kept him from losing his colors.

Nate wasn't afraid to die. *Death's just what happens when you're done living.*

He stared at Owen's closed eyes through the flickering light. Nate might not be afraid, but he definitely didn't want to go out lying helpless and weak beside Owen.

As Jared finished sewing, they listened to the steady rhythm of the needle and thread lacing its way through Owen's skin. Rob breathed heavily beside them, peering over Jared's shoulder.

Finally, Jared sat up, leaning back on his haunches. He ran a hand over his thin blond mustache. "He's ready. Keep him hydrated." He packed away the kit. "And keep an eye on the wound. Don't let anything happen to him. We'll be back sometime tomorrow with the doc and some meds."

"Sure."

The wooden floor creaked as Jared went into the other room and returned with Nate's blanket.

Great.

"Make sure he doesn't get too hot tomorrow when it starts warming up."

Nate swallowed his disgust as his blanket fell over Owen.

Jared blew out the candles on the countertop and the room darkened, leaving only the dull light from the one on the low table.

"Later," Rob said. The door clicked as the guys pulled it closed behind them.

Nate stared at the ceiling. He could go back to his room, but he knew the instructions. He'd need to make sure Owen made it. Owen's black hair was matted to his face, the candle casting shadows over his round, pale cheeks.

Not so smug now, eh? Nate lay down beside him, pulled the edge of the blanket over himself, and closed his eyes. If Owen lived through the night, Nate might just kill him.

* * *

Nate slowly became aware of the light filtering in through the window and of the sound of ragged, uneven breathing beside him. *Still alive.*

A thin line of perspiration lined Owen's upper lip and a bead of sweat ran down his forehead. Nate pictured himself smothering him with the palm of his hand. It wouldn't be hard. Nobody would see him. He could claim Owen died in the night.

He stood, wincing as he put a little weight on his bad leg to warm it up. Killing Owen would be pointless. Dangerous, too, considering how close Owen and Jared were. No, Jared expected

Nate to keep him alive. And Marshall would expect Nate to do what he was told, especially when Jared was the one doing the telling.

He limped across to the cupboard and grabbed one of the small, yellow plastic cups he'd inherited with the place. It used to belong to a child, he assumed. The former residents were already gone when the Grims awarded him this address, but he'd only switched from the glass dishes to the plastic ones shortly after his injury, when he'd discovered how uncoordinated he was with only one working hand.

Blowing out the dust that had settled inside the cup, he made his way through to the other room. He was still weak. It didn't help that he kept his water in the farthest corner of his apartment. Sitting beside the full bucket, he dipped his cup into it, then drank. The water splashed over his dry lips, some running down his chin, but most of it cooling his parched throat. He leaned his head against the wall, closing his eyes. He'd have to bring Owen some of the water. It would have made things easier if he kept it in the other room, but he liked to keep his valuables as far away from the entrance as possible. The X on the door would keep most people out but, if anyone chanced a robbery, he wanted his water out of reach.

The room was so quiet he considered letting himself drift off for a moment. Sleep would feel so good right now. His eyes opened and he turned his head towards the doorway, listening. Nothing.

That's not right. It was too quiet. He couldn't hear Owen breathing anymore.

"Owen!" He scrambled to his feet. He dropped the cup beside the bucket and ran as best he could through the room to where Owen's body lay on the floor. He dropped to his knees and his heart sank as he stared down at Owen's still, expressionless face. He placed his fingers hard on his neck but, even as he did, he knew what he'd find. He steadied himself, tuning out his own pounding heart and concentrating instead on finding a rhythm beneath his fingertips. Nothing.

Owen had won after all. "You had to mess me up one last time."

CHAPTER 4

Nate's eyes traveled down the length of Owen's torso, noticing, for the first time, the deep red stain across the blanket that covered them both during the night. He wasn't sure if it had been an infection or the seeping of blood through the stitches, but Owen was gone.

Death's just what happens when you're done living. He looked away from Owen and out the window into the light. He'd seen death too many times to count, but it always seemed strange to him how people's faces seemed to change when life was no longer in them. Some of the guys in his crew held on to some vague hope of an afterlife. *See you on the other side.*

And Trevor actually *believed* in a God and a heaven—and probably a hell, too. But if there was a hell, they were living in it now. It was better not to think about death, but it was hard to ignore it when he spent the night beside a guy on his way out.

Death is just what happens...

He saw the two bikes from down the street before he heard them; Jared's blond head was just visible at the end of the street. He was moving quickly and Nate knew the doctor would be with him. Rob was likely patrolling on his own, which worked in Nate's favor. It would be an easier fight, if it came down to it. He knew what they were going to think.

Nate struggled to his feet, distancing himself from the body. He pulled open the door just as Jared jogged up the apartment steps, carrying his bike. It clattered to the floor as Jared dropped to his knees beside Owen's body. The doctor, panting heavily, his thinning black hair matted with sweat, dismounted on the sidewalk. Nate turned back to Jared as the older man wrestled his bike up the steps.

"What did you do?" Jared asked, still looking at Owen.

"Nothing." Nate readied himself.

Jared slowly stood. His thin lips were pulled into a hard line, his small eyes narrowed to near slits. "Did you kill him?" His voice was quiet.

Not a good sign. "No."

"He was alive when we left."

Nate met Jared's gaze. "Barely."

"You didn't like him."

"Nope."

"This would have been a good time to get back at him."

"Nah. It wouldn't make sense." He forced himself to relax, wishing he had his piece on him. Even with one arm, he was pretty sure he could take Jared, but a gun would make it so much cleaner. He shrugged, motioning with his chin to the blood-stained blanket. "He bled out during the night." Nate left out the part about finding him alive in the morning. The simpler, the better. He couldn't come off as defensive, especially if he didn't want to have to kill Jared. He'd pretty much guarantee his own execution if he did. *And I'd have to kill the doctor, too.*

He glanced at the stocky older man who was doubled

over with his hands on his knees, trying to catch his breath. He couldn't leave any witnesses.

"You were supposed to watch him," Jared said.

"I seriously tried."

"Pretty sure you won't lose sleep over it." Jared nodded towards the doctor. "Wrap him up, Doc. I'll go for a wagon. We're going to have to pull him out to the site."

They'd stopped burying the bodies now. They would burn him with the others. Jared walked past Nate and through the door without another word. Nate tried to read his face as he passed. It was stone.

The doctor, wringing his hands, crouched down over the body. He checked for a pulse with shaky fingers. After a moment, he leaned back on his haunches, sighed, then stared down at Owen's pale body.

"Hurry up," Nate said, nudging the doctor with his toe. "Jared's going to want him ready when he gets back."

The doc stood, then began wrapping the body in the top blanket. Not like Nate wanted it back now anyway.

The doctor groaned as he rolled the body towards the door.

"So, Doc, bet you never pictured this when you signed up for med school, hey?" Nate said it as payback for the blanket but, when the doctor just stared down at the body, he added, "You're glad to be of service, though, right? Really making a difference."

The doctor pushed the body against the wall and straightened, watching for Jared from the window. Trying to ignore Nate. Not a chance.

"Maybe you pictured white walls and clean tables and big paychecks? But, hey, riding bicycles and wrapping dead guys in cheap cotton's not too bad, right?" Nate grinned. "Wonder what's worse. That your money's completely useless now, or that people like me own you?"

The doctor said nothing. It was kind of impressive, considering how much the doctor must hate them. Nate figured the doctors must feel like it was bad enough that all three of the small city hospitals had burnt down, that they had almost no medical supplies to work with, that most people they treated would die of infection anyway. But to be put to work by the gangs—serving Members and criminals and kids that some of them wouldn't even have looked twice at in their medical practice—was a complete loss of power. Nate wished the doctor would say something so he could put him back in his place.

"He's coming down the street now," was all the doctor finally said. Nate's leg had gone stiff with pain again. "Are you going to help me with this?"

Nate wanted to refuse, but there was no way the heavyset man could lug that body down the stairs on his own. Somehow, he didn't think Jared would approve. Jared Ward was practically a sociopath, but he looked out for the few friends he had.

"Fine," Nate said. It wasn't the first time he'd helped move a body. He grabbed Owen's feet with his good arm, letting the doctor struggle with his shoulders. "Got him?" They leveled the body. The doctor grunted. Nate backed out the door, going slowly enough to allow the heavier man to follow him without losing his grip on Owen.

"Be easier if rigor'd started to set in," Nate said quietly, getting in a final jab before they reached Jared. The people who used to save lives before all of this seemed to have an especially hard time dealing with the aftermath of so much death.

"Lay him here," Jared said, still straddling his bike. Behind it, tied by rough cords of salvaged rope, were the remnants of a front door, makeshift straps hanging loosely off the sides. He'd brought the big one. Only the best for Owen.

* * *

That night, Nate sat on his bed in his darkened apartment, trying to massage the feeling back into his leg. Owen's body had been heavy, and the muscle spasms were worse than usual. Trevor, he knew, would be on his way over already, and the thought of his pity was enough to make him sick. He looked down at his leg, willing the pain still shooting up from his heel to subside.

He held his breath, listening for Trevor. Aside from the sounds of the city, there was nothing. His crew wouldn't be patrolling this street until later in the night, and he knew Jared wouldn't be back for a while. Once the body had been strapped tight to the door, Nate had watched Jared and Owen disappear down the street, the doctor trailing behind them. He grinned again when he pictured the doctor's pale face, but only for a moment. The doctor was weak, but at least he was whole.

Nate glanced at his useless hand.

The quiet whir of tires on pavement signaled a single rider. Trevor. He forced himself up, gritting his teeth against the pain.

The front door eased open, the creak of the hinges giving away Trevor's entrance.

"Coop? You here?" The whisper carried through the mostly empty space.

Nate heard the thump of the bike as Trevor rested it up against the wall.

"Fell asleep waiting for you," Nate said. The candle at the coffee table had already burned low, so what he said could have been the truth. That he'd been sitting on the bed in a cold sweat since the others had left was something he'd die before admitting.

"Brought the map." Trevor quickly crossed the room, pulling a large, rolled-up paper from his backpack.

Nate eased himself down to the floor by the edge of the low table.

Trevor knelt on the floor across the table from him, unrolled the map, and flattened it. "We'll make a plan tonight and then go back and see the girl in a couple of days."

"Tomorrow," Nate said.

Trevor's eyebrows shot up. "You're really not going to give her an extra day?"

"What do you think?"

"Fine." He gestured to the map. "The route's the same this week?"

"Yeah. They won't make any changes until the end of the month."

"And they still don't know about that?" He pointed to a small community Nate had circled for him weeks ago.

"No. They still think it's empty. After the fires, the whole neighborhood there looked pretty uninhabitable."

"Thanks again for hooking that up for me. If you hadn't told me people were moving back in—if you hadn't kept it from your crew—it could have been *my* bike that girl found."

Nate shrugged. "As long as you give me my cut, we're good." He kept his eyes on the map, tracing a route with his finger. "Remember to watch for the patrols here, though, when you're with the girl. From sunset to sunrise, four rotations."

"Right." Trevor was quiet for a moment as they looked at the map. He cleared his throat. "John Ashwood would help you, you know." His voice was almost a whisper.

"Careful," Nate said. It was bad enough he was working with an Independent—even if that Independent was his oldest and maybe only friend—but to even *mention* the name of that guy … it was a betrayal even Nate could barely stomach. "Two of our guys got strung up last week because of him."

"Not because of him," Trevor said. "He was trying to help them get out."

"Enough. I'm okay helping you, Trev, but we don't talk about John. Not unless you're turning him in."

"Fine." Trevor raised his palms in surrender. "Fine. Show me the patrol route again."

* * *

Later, Nate peered out the dark window as Trevor pulled away. He could barely make him out in the moonlight, a mere shadowed figure on a bike. One of these days, Trevor would be caught.

Death's just what happens when you're done living, Nate thought.

He held his breath, listening. No shots or shouts. Trevor was in the clear for now.

Nate slid his Glock into the waistband of his jeans and slipped out the door. His leg protested but he ignored it. Just because the girl was buying herself some time didn't mean he couldn't use that extra time productively. It took a few seconds for his eyes to adjust to the darkness but, soon enough, the buildings were more than just shapes in the night. He walked the familiar route to her place. He wasn't exactly invisible, but his uneven gait announced who he was. Despite his limp, nobody messed with him. Partially because he was still a Grim. Partially because he was good with a gun and he could use his one hand with extreme force.

As he neared her place, he slowed. It wouldn't do any good to have her hear him approaching and get spooked. At her apartment, he winced as he attempted a crouch. No good. Shifting, he sat beside the rectangle window, his legs stretched out in front of him and his back against the brick wall. It was dark inside, quiet too. They could have packed up already, disappeared. He should have forced the issue when he saw her. Taken some insurance. He should have—

A small, shrill voice rose from the low apartment beside him. "I don't hear anything, Robyn."

"Shhh," a voice hissed back.

So they had heard him after all. They were listening for him now. He grinned. They'd almost had him convinced they'd cut out. He fought the temptation to pop his head in, to give them a scare. Instead, he closed his eyes and focused on his breathing. Slow, soft, inaudible. After a moment, there was movement from inside. Someone was crossing the room, feet padding across the floor towards the window. He could almost feel her, standing there and peering out into the darkness. She wouldn't see him, not unless she stuck her head out—and she didn't seem the type to do something so risky. Then again, she'd taken the bike. He turned his head, angling his view towards the window.

"He said he wouldn't come until tomorrow—" the young girl started again.

"Sam!" Her voice was right beside him, loud enough to carry clearly through the window and down the street. If she hadn't given herself away already, she would have now. Maybe she wasn't such a sure thing after all.

"Robyn." It had to be the old woman speaking. "Nobody's out there. Come back to bed."

"I don't trust him, Meredith."

"You're the one who made the deal with him. We can still—"

"No. We keep the deal as long as we need it. Just ..." There was a silence, and she sighed heavily. "Just watch out for him."

Nate listened for her to cross the room again, but she didn't, not for a long time.

By the time her footfalls went back across the room and were followed by the quiet groan of the bedspring, the cold of the pavement had seeped through his jeans and he was fighting to keep his teeth from chattering. He hadn't expected to be stuck outside of her apartment for so long, but she'd stood there so stubbornly, listening for him. He'd had no choice but to wait.

Point for the girl, he thought.

Not that it had been a complete waste of time, of course. He got to his feet, balancing on his good leg while he waited for feeling to return to the other one. She'd been waiting because she was trying to protect her little family, which meant, of course, they would be the key to keeping her in check. He started back down the darkened alleyway. In some ways, he guessed he envied her. She had something to lose.

CHAPTER 5

Robyn waited by the window, alone, her bike propped up against the bed beside her. The sun had set ages ago, and it had been two days since she'd seen Trevor and Nate. She knew there was no way Nate would let her get away with naming the terms. He'd come today.

Sure enough, Nate's familiar sneakers appeared in the window. He lifted the glass and hopped down.

Trevor leaned in, too. "If you don't mind, I'm going to stay out here with the bike. If we're just on our way out, there's no reason to toss it down there again. Can you hurry? I'm feeling a little exposed."

"You sure you're not going to get me killed?" she called up to him.

"I'm still alive, aren't I?" Trevor said. "I know this city like I know myself … and I know myself pretty well, in case you were wondering. Members aren't everywhere. I have their routes pretty well memorized, thanks to Coop here."

"If Coop … if Nate has you, what does he need me for?"

"Coop doesn't *have* me." His voice hardened slightly. "I

mean, I won't let him starve. But Coop still wears their colors." He glanced back towards Nate. "He tells me that you're going to ride anyway and, if I don't help you out here, I'm kind of getting you killed. So here I am."

"Out of the goodness of your heart?"

"Something like that."

She lifted her bike from the wall, trying to make a decision. She didn't see how she could put them off anymore. And something about Trevor told her she could trust him, at least for now.

"Fine," she finally said, "but Nate needs to go … wherever he goes. Crawl back into the hole he slithered out of."

She walked towards the window. Nate gestured towards her, obviously aiming to help her with the bike. She pulled it away. Struggling to lift the bike up to the window, she was suddenly aware of how much upper body strength these guys must have and how much training she had ahead of her if she were actually going to make a go of this. The bike fell down again.

"Some help?" she called, and Trevor reached through the opening to help her.

Nate grabbed the bike's frame and passed it up to Trevor, who pulled it through.

She turned to Nate. "Out."

"You sure you don't want me to hang around and keep my eye on the girls?"

She crossed her arms, staring at the window.

"Suit yourself," he said.

When she joined the guys on the street, Nate was resting his arms on the handlebars, the front tire between his knees. "This really is a beauty." He straightened as she moved to take her bike back. "You hit it big when you found this one."

"I guess we'll see."

"Let me know how it goes," he said, backing away. "I'll come by tomorrow."

He saluted her, then silently turned and limped down the street, tucking in close to the building. His body was damaged, but somehow he exuded strength.

As he disappeared in the distance, she turned to Trevor, who stood beside his bike.

"Ready to ride?" Trevor swung his leg over the bar and straddled the bike, his left foot resting on his pedal. It was difficult to tell the make or even the color in the dark, but the thick frame and heavy tread told her it was sturdy.

"Nice bike," she asked, stalling. She used to love cycling back home. Trail riding, city riding—a bike meant freedom. She guessed it meant freedom here, too, especially for the Independents. But the stakes were so much higher now.

"Yup. Full suspension. She's not as quiet in the city as your hard tail there with the road slicks, but she's great when the streets are bad or when I need to cut through somewhere."

"Where did you get her, um, it?"

"It's mine from before the blackout. Still have my helmet and gloves at home ... but, you know, we can't wear those anymore. Makes you a target." He half-smiled. "Anyway, four years ago, when I was fifteen, I joined this inner city cycling club. It was probably what kept me out of the gang back when Coop joined. Neither of us had it great at home." He stopped.

She shouldn't be letting him tell her all this stuff. Too personal. She looked at her hands, gripping her bike.

He cleared his throat. "The Grims gave Coop the family he never had. I found mine at the club. The bike was donated, actually. It used to be too big for me." She couldn't help but notice how his body seemed made for that bike. "I'd say I've grown into it."

She looked back down the dark street. "You guys grew up here?"

"Yup."

"Where's the rest of your family? Your real family?"

"We were in the North End." He said it like that explained it all. "Everything was so close together there and the fires moved so quickly. Heard the suburbs weren't much better. Listen, I know you're scared, but we need to get moving. Trust me, you'll be fine."

Sharing was over. Was she relieved?

"It's dark, but it's bright enough to see where we're going. Your eyes adjust. You'll memorize the route soon enough." Trevor pushed one foot down now and his bike surged forward. She scrambled onto her own and followed. He was right about the sound; his tires crunched over the fine gravel along the road as he headed off through the night. The noise from her own slicks added to his. They were broadcasting their ride.

"Hurry," he whispered back to her, and she closed the gap between them. "We need to get out of here. There's a friendlier neighborhood not far ahead."

She trailed him across the main street. He pedaled hard, leaning forward. They crossed over to the next back lane. She cringed at a deep, hacking cough from the gutter as they passed, but nobody was following them. Her fingers were already stiff with cold on the handlebars. Autumn was bad. Winter would be worse.

She followed Trevor down a small walking path between the buildings, feeling blind in the narrow passageway. As it opened to another street, she drifted her bike in closer to the wall. He'd already done the same. Her breath came in shorter bursts. Exhaustion began to set in. She'd always been athletic, but the lack of food and constant hiding had obviously affected her. In some way, she was relieved to have something to focus on other than the terror of being spotted. She knew they were harder to see at night, and getting a clean shot was unlikely in the dark. Of course, that she was riding right now was evidence it wasn't completely impossible.

Her legs ached, and her lungs burned as she gasped for more air. She wished she'd asked him to walk the route with her first so she could get to know it a little. The Grims would be watching for people casing routes, though, so maybe it was good she hadn't bothered.

The distance between them grew, and she felt a quick flash of panic. What if she lost him? Worse still—what if he intentionally left her behind?

She picked up her pace, forcing her body to fall in line, trying to close the gap between them. It wasn't working. She had no idea where they were now. She'd been so focused on following him she'd totally lost track of where they were going. What if he weren't trying to lose her? What if he were simply trying to disorient her? She'd followed this stranger, and left Nate back there. With her family.

She slowed down, coming to a stop and finally glancing around at her surroundings. She tried to catch her breath. The moon lit up a few of the small, squat houses lining the street beside her. They weren't as close together as the apartments in her neighborhood but the area still didn't seem like it was ever one of wealth. The homes were in various stages of decay from the fires and from vandals. She was directly in front of a house with smashed windows and a door that hung loosely from the hinges.

Inside was, of course, black. Someone could be standing in the doorway, looking out at her, for all she could tell.

Shivering suddenly, she rolled forward, stopping her bike in the gap between the structures. She stood, paralyzed with fear and indecision. The sound of approaching tires filled the quiet and, before she had time to make any sort of decision, Trevor pulled up beside her, his face close enough for her to see his concern.

"What happened?" he asked. "Are you hurt?"

She shook her head, still winded. "No," she finally said. "You were too fast, and I don't know where we are."

"We're a few miles north of Smith," he said. "I can draw you a map in the daylight so you can find it again. It's amazing. The fires pretty much wiped everything out here. There was so much damage. Even the buildings that were still standing were unsafe. They'd just collapse, no warning, nothing. Nobody stayed here. The whole neighborhood was completely empty. Grims raided the place and wrote it off. But, after a while, people started coming back. They brought what they had, or could find—which wasn't much—and they made this place a home. The Members haven't been back yet, so it's a good place to work."

"If it's so great, why don't you just move in here?"

"I'm an Independent. If I were caught here, they'd be implicated."

"And you care because?" Her voice sounded harsher than she'd meant it to, but she figured it was a fair enough question. Why should he care what happened to a bunch of strangers?

He shrugged, palms up. "Because we're all still human, aren't we?"

Were they, though? Really? "So, what now?"

"Now you come with me. I have a few trades for some

customers, and I'm looking to find a few new ones, too." He pushed off.

"If this is your route, what am I doing here? Are we partners now?"

"No. Not partners. Nate has another area for me. Less secure than this one, more risk. But it's bigger, so bigger payoff. The plan is to teach you this one and then move on myself."

She nodded. She was definitely into less risk. He started out again and she could tell he was making an effort to slow it down a little. Even so, he was quick, and she concentrated on pushing down and then lifting up again in a steady rhythm. She remembered the luxury of riding clipped-in at home. When her cleated cycling shoes were locked into the pedal, her foot and leg felt like part of her bicycle, moving almost effortlessly.

Her eyes suddenly stung. She'd never really mourned the loss of her bike. Of all the things there were to miss, it hadn't even registered on her radar. *Don't care. Don't care.* But somehow, she did. She'd rode competitively back then, starting with her BMX, then moving on to mountain biking and then to cyclocross. But, like swimming lessons and dance class and high school, she'd written her bike off as one of those things that no longer existed as part of her reality.

She remembered it now, though. The way the air had felt on her cheeks, the way her muscles burned as she pushed them past breaking, the way it felt to ride the berm in perfect control of her body and bike. Blinking, she picked up her pace, pulling in tight behind Tyler, just short of drafting. They turned to cut across a small park and she forced herself to ignore the fact they were out in the open. Instead, she focused on the way her tire ate up the grass in front of her and on keeping her front wheel from buzzing Trevor's.

***

"Come out, come out, wherever you are!" Nate called, his voice echoing against the bare walls of the small basement apartment.

Robyn clearly wanted him to believe she'd sent the old woman and the girl away somewhere. After the two bikers had disappeared into the darkness, he'd let himself into her place. There was no way she'd actually gotten rid of them. His recon the other night had made that clear enough. She needed them. Family, or something like that. Pulling his lighter from his pocket, he lit the small candle they had sitting on the table. They had to be in here. Somewhere.

"Sam? Meredith? I know you're in here." Again, the information he'd gleaned sitting outside their place was helpful. "I know Robyn doesn't trust me, but I'm not a bad guy." *Well, not all the time, anyway.* He peered into the little bathroom off the main room. The small shower, with its yellowed tiles and rusted metal drain, and the off-white toilet were relics of another time. He peered into the dry bowl and lifted the lid of the tank. He used his for storage now, but hers was empty. The flowered wallpaper in this room was peeling, and a faded outline told him where there had once been cupboards. Robyn—or someone before her—had likely traded them last winter or used them for firewood.

He walked through the main room again and grinned as he noticed the flat closet door behind the bed. It wasn't unusual to have furniture pushed up against closet or crawl spaces—made it harder for people to make a quick getaway with your stuff— but he knew that was where they were hiding. He pushed the bed away from the entrance. They would be listening to the frame scrape across the floor and know he was coming. When he opened that door, would they blow him away? He hesitated, hand on the door. Done in by a kid and an old lady. It wasn't impossible. People were capable of anything.

"I'm coming in," he called through the door. "I'm not going to hurt you." Taking a breath, he pulled open the closet door and blinked in surprise. Boxes were stacked up nearly to the top of the closet. There was no way they were in here. Unless … Of course!

He pulled the boxes clear. They were light—probably empty, more or less. All a show.

"Ready or not, here I come!" he called into the large hole in the wall.

When he stepped through the opening, it was completely black inside, although he could smell smoke. A candle must be smoldering somewhere. He stepped away from the entrance and waited for his eyes to adjust to the dark, the candlelight from the other room affording him just enough luminance to begin to make out shapes. A small bed in one corner—and two people pressed against the wall in the other.

"Listen, the smell in here is even worse than out there," he said. "Might as well come out now. I'm not going to hurt you—promise." *Not yet, anyway.* Not unless he needed to.

"What do you want?" the old woman asked. She spoke quickly, loudly, but she couldn't keep the tremor from the last word.

"To keep you safe," he said. "If I can find you, anyone can. You're safer out where I can keep an eye on you."

"Why do you care if we're safe?" the little one—Sam—whispered. Her voice cracked. She must've been crying.

"Maybe I'm just a nice person," he said. When they answered with silence, he chuckled. "Okay, maybe not. But I bet, if something happens to you, my deal with Robyn is off. And nobody wants that."

The quiet stretched for a little longer and then the shadows shifted away from the wall.

"I hate it in here anyway," Sam said, her voice steadier.

He stepped back as they passed him. He followed. He could imagine Robyn's face when she saw her little family sitting with him. It would be a good reminder of what she had to lose.

Meredith and Sam waited for him against the far wall in the main room. He couldn't see their expressions in the dim candlelight, but he could sense their fear.

"Relax," he said, sitting at the table with his back to them. "You're probably safer with me than you've ever been." He reached into his pocket with his good hand. "A game." He didn't need these two getting jumpy. He pulled the cards from their fitted cardboard box and cut the deck. "You're not planning to spend all night over there, are you?" He shuffled the stacks together.

"No." Again it was Sam who gave in as she moved away from the wall.

"Samantha …" Meredith said, but Sam was already at the table, sitting across from him. Now that she was closer, he could see that her little face was all serious as she studied him. "What are those?"

"These?" He held the cards up. Of course, she'd never seen cards. They were a luxury. Most people would have traded them for necessities or burned them for heat. "How old are you?"

"Old enough."

He snorted, then leaned towards her. "Obviously not, or you would know what these are."

"They're cards," Meredith said, taking the empty chair and sitting at the table. "You play games with them."

"What kind of games?" Sam asked.

Nate shrugged. "All sorts." He'd never had to explain something so simple. "Mostly to do with numbers. You know your numbers?"

"'Course I do. Meri taught me to read this summer."

"With books?"

"What else?" Sam asked.

Books. Nate shook his head. Cards were rare, but books … nobody hung on to books. The gangs had raided all the libraries that hadn't burnt to the ground. They had used up every page for fuel last winter.

"Why'd she teach you to read?" he asked.

"Because we're not animals yet."

Nate wanted to laugh, but his voice stuck in his throat. Not animals? Then again, maybe she was onto something. He wasn't sure animals were capable of the sick cruelty people were—even before the blackout. "How'd you end up with books?"

Meredith answered his question. "When my house caught fire and I had to leave, I took them with me."

"And your fearless leader was okay with you keeping them?"

"If you mean Robyn, it wasn't up to her," she said. "And, anyway, by the time we met, books weren't worth much as trade anymore. We did okay last winter with what we had. I suspect the subject will be up for discussion again when the first snow falls."

"Would you let her burn them?"

The silence stretched. She finally cleared her throat. "Yes. These chairs would go first. But then, if we truly needed to, I would give up my books."

"Besides," Sam added, "we almost have them memorized by now anyway. Meri only brought three."

"Which three?

"There's one about a family on an island." Sam counted on her fingers. "And one's about a magical land. And one's about God."

"About God." He looked at Meredith. "Don't tell me it's the Bible. Thought you said you'd burn it if you had to."

"It's not the pages that matter. It's what's in them. And I've got most of it up here." She tapped her head. "And in here." She laid her hand on her chest.

He laughed. "You can't be serious." She was worse than Trevor, and *he* was crazy.

"Don't laugh." Sam's small, sharp voice rose a few decibels. "I believe her. *Meredith* never lies. Are you going to teach me cards, or what?"

Still grinning, he held up his hands in surrender. He had to give her credit. She was pretty brave … for a kid.

"Okay," he said, dealing. "Let's start with Poker."

CHAPTER 6

Trevor veered sharply to the right and Robyn struggled to follow. After a slight incline, they pulled out of the park. More small, broken houses lined the street, and he slowed as he approached the end of it. She matched his pace, coming up alongside him as they halted. They walked their bikes up a short path and stopped at an entranceway. The door was gone. They could have walked right in, but Trevor knocked once on the frame. After a few seconds, a boy came to the door. His footsteps had been so quiet she hadn't even heard him approaching. He looked like he couldn't be more than a few years older than Sam—maybe eight or nine at the most.

He stood up straight, his shoulders squared and his back rigid. "You bring it?"

"'Course," Trevor answered, pulling off his backpack. "You said you had first aid supplies?"

The boy nodded, handing him a small tube of some sort of ointment and a thick roll of bandages. "That's for the inhaler." He placed another roll in Trevor's palm. "And that's for you."

"Pleasure, as always," Trevor said, shoving the goods into his backpack. He took out a blue inhaler and handed it to the boy. "How's your mom?"

"She's doing a little better now that it's colder. It's the worst when seasons change."

"I'll keep my eyes open for more. Tell your mom I'm praying for her."

"Always do." The boy lifted his hand in a quick wave before he turned and disappeared into the dark house.

"Come on." Trevor motioned Robyn with his head as he mounted his bike again. Was that what Sam looked like to outsiders? Hard and cold like that boy?

A young couple came to the door at their next stop, a baby's wail echoing from somewhere inside. They had two cans of food to trade for a few Amoxicillin capsules.

"Sorry it took me so long," Trevor said, handing her the pills. "There's not much of this out there."

The woman's eyes welled up when she saw the small pills. He handed the medication to her and she disappeared back inside the house.

"Thank you for finding that," the man whispered, thrusting the two tins at Trevor.

Trevor took both, and then, as the man turned to go, reached out and touched his shoulder. When the man turned, Trevor handed one of the cans back. "I owe one to a customer. But I was late, so …" He shrugged.

Robyn gasped as the man, clutching the can with one hand, lunged out and hugged Trevor with the other, before disappearing into the house.

"Did you know him?" she asked as they got back on their bikes.

"Not really. Just from the route. But they needed it, didn't they?"

"What about you?"

"I do all right."

She wanted to tell him it wouldn't actually save that couple or their baby. That a can of food and a couple pills couldn't last forever and, if it took him so long this time, what made him think he'd find any more out there? She bit her tongue. She didn't need to state the obvious.

A small candle lit up in a window ahead. It was the signal for a courier, the same as they used for the Members. The gangs didn't usually do night deliveries but, every now and then, when it was light enough and they were looking to make some extra profit, they answered. It made sense that the people who used the Independents would use the same signal; it was safer for everyone if the Members thought the call was for them. Of course, people probably weren't picky about who answered the call. They were just trying to survive.

"This one's a new customer, right?" she called softly to him.

"Yup. We'll see what they need and what they're willing to trade."

As they approached the doorway, Trevor put his hand on her arm. "Hang back here," he said. "I don't know them yet. It's safer if you stay ready." His voice was calm, but she didn't miss the weight of his words.

He made his way up the walk, and she took a couple of steps back. She would have liked to tell herself she wasn't sure what she'd do if he got in any kind of trouble, but, in reality, she knew. Her hands gripped her handlebars and she stayed straddling the bike, already angled away from the house towards the street.

She couldn't see who came to the door, but whoever it was didn't seem to pose any threat. Trevor and the person talked quietly. Trevor took a small notepad from his pocket, and a small flame sparked to life. Leaning the pad against the doorframe, he handed the lighter to the person at the door who held it up for him. He scribbled down something, took the lighter back, and pulled his bike around.

"Look alive," he said as they started out again. "You okay for a few more stops? I want to cover about three more blocks tonight."

She nodded. "I'm fine."

He moved slower now, and the lack of Grim presence felt freeing. The idea they could ever be safe from gang control was foreign to her. She knew her body would be complaining in the morning but, for now, she felt *alive*.

It was still dark when they turned to head home. Trevor's backpack had been emptied and filled already, and he had a list of things he needed to search for and another list of items people were hoping to trade. He wasn't pushing her as hard now, and they were still in the safe-zone.

"There are only so many hours," he said as they cut across the park together. "You get a feel for when morning's coming even when you can't see it yet. Getting caught at dawn a few times in the Smith Street area, trying to find somewhere to stash your bike so you don't get caught with it, teaches you to pay attention. You need to watch the moon and the color of the sky."

Partway through the park, he pulled his brakes and his bike came to a slow stop.

She drew up beside him. "What's wrong? Why did we stop?"

"Look around at this place," he said.

Her eyes swept the area. The black outlines of oak trees stood out along the edges of the park, and the long grass was knee-deep. They'd stopped almost directly beside a tall set of monkey bars. She knew, without seeing, the paint would be gone, long burnt and worn off. The bars themselves were partially twisted. Beside it stood two poles from which hung two empty chains.

"This used to be a place where kids played. Can you believe that little kids now might not even recognize a park if they saw one?"

She knew her parents used to take Sam to the one by their house all the time. It was unlikely her sister would even remember it now. "What's your point?"

"It's just … every time I cross this spot, I think, maybe someday, things *will* change if enough people want it bad enough. It's why I ride, you know. Maybe it's why you want to."

"Maybe. I don't know. Even if it's true, the problem is people don't want it bad enough. *I* don't want it bad enough. I just want to keep my family safe."

"But over here, away from the Members—can't you feel it? How everything's different?" He was so earnest she was almost sorry for him.

"Why are you still helping Nate?" she asked, instead of answering. It didn't make any sense to her, especially now, after seeing Trevor's selflessness and naive hope.

He shrugged. "You don't know him. Coop hasn't always been … like he is. And sometimes, when his guard is down, I see the guy he used to be. But even if that guy were completely gone, I'd still help him."

"Why?"

"Because he's my friend."

She rolled her eyes. *Right.* "Think we can get going now?"

They started out again. She could tell he was disappointed. He had wanted her to see it like he did. To have faith in people, to have faith in Nate. But faith wasn't something she had a lot of use for. She followed him through the narrow passageway again.

"You know the way home from here?" he asked.

"Think so."

"Great. See you next time." He half-saluted her. "I'll send Coop to let you know where to meet. Not exactly comfortable riding around here."

Without another word, Trevor veered off and disappeared into the darkness, the steady sound of his bike fading. She was alone, and her bike, signifying freedom less than an hour ago, now made her a target. She wanted nothing more than to get home and get off it. As she reached the apartment, she hopped off her bike and ran alongside it. With a quick glance around, she pulled the window bars and shoved the bike through the window. She jumped down, almost landing on top of it, and slammed the window shut. Her heart pounded in her ears. She was home. She was safe.

"How was it?" Sam asked from beside her.

She whipped around, noticing the dimly lit space. Sam, Meredith, and Nate sat at the table. Nate. What was he still doing there? *I'm gonna be sick.*

"Learn anything useful?" Nate asked, looking up at her from his hand of cards. She couldn't read his expression in the low light, but he sounded smug.

"Get out," she said.

"We're in the middle of a game," he said. "Thought these ladies could use something to do. Nobody was sleeping, anyway."

She steadied her gaze on Meredith, who suddenly seemed overly interested in her cards. "I told you not to come out."

"It wasn't her fault," Sam said. "He found us."

Her stomach turned upside down. If he found them, *anyone* could find them. Her clever hiding place—all the work breaking through the wall, hiding the hole behind boxes in the closet—seemed childish. Finally, she asked him, "Why?"

"Well, I knew they'd be hiding in here somewhere, probably terrified, wondering what happened." His voice was artificially light. He was obviously bragging. He could've found them any time he wanted. She wasn't in control. "So I thought I would do you a favor."

"Please don't do me any … favors." She shoved the bed behind them away from the wall, its legs grinding across the floor. They'd put the bed back but left the boxes stacked beside it. "I'm trying to keep them safe. Mostly from you."

"I can keep them safe. We're partners now, right?"

She couldn't look at him. She said nothing as she wheeled the bike through the opening and leaned it on the wall in the nearly empty room. When she came back in, she glanced down at the cards. What kind of game was he really playing? She stacked the boxes back up and pulled the bed back into place.

"Full house!" Sam clapped her hands.

"What, you some kind of card shark here?" he asked, his tone playful. He'd taught her little sister Poker but, for some reason, it bothered Robyn less than it should have. Playing cards was something to keep Sam's mind sharp and occupied, besides the books. No, what bothered her was the idea of him sitting with her family, tricking them into trusting him.

"Well, I'm home now, so you can go," Robyn said.

He smirked. "Don't you want to sleep? I could watch them for you."

"I said get out." She kept her voice even.

"We're in the middle of a game," Sam said, turning to look up at her. "Could we finish at least? Please? I'm having *fun*, Robyn." Fun. Like Trevor's big dreams.

She wanted to snatch the stupid cards away and throw them at Nate's self-satisfied face, but she just couldn't do it. "What are you playing for?" she asked instead.

"Buttons," Sam replied.

"Where'd you get buttons?"

"Nate brought them."

Nate. Of course. "Aren't you just the picture of generosity?"

"They're buttons," he said flatly. "Believe it or not, they're not exactly a hot commodity on the market right now."

"Please?" Sam asked again.

"Fine. Just until you finish the game. Then he leaves."

They murmured agreement, and she settled onto the bed to watch them. She pulled the covers over her legs, which were suddenly cold. She'd let him stay until they finished their game, and she'd watch them until he was gone. She wouldn't sleep, not until he was safely out of there, not until … She didn't get a chance to finish the thought. Within seconds, her body's need for sleep overcame her will.

***

When Robyn opened her eyes, the first thing she noticed was the light. She could tell it must be past noon; the sun filtered in through the window above her. The second thing was that she was alone.

Sitting upright in bed, she pushed her hair out of her eyes. "Sam?" She stood. "Meredith!" She crossed the small space, then leaned out the window. Why had she let herself fall asleep, especially when Nate was still there?

She pulled herself out of the room. *Where would they go?*

She could think of only one place. Running around the corner of the building to the fire escape, she jumped to grab the ledge of the half-ladder hanging down. Anyone strong enough had access, and sometimes predators would make their way up, but it was such an effort with nothing much to be gained that usually people didn't bother. On the first platform, she leaned back and tried to see up onto the roof.

"Sam!" she called.

There was no response.

She continued up the escape, stopping at each set of windows to peer in. It was almost black inside each one, with the adjacent building blocking most of the light. "Sam!" As she ran along the platform, the metal clanged under her feet and swayed slightly with her weight. If they weren't up there, she'd have no idea where else to look. And if Nate took them—if she'd accidentally let Nate take them—she didn't know how she could survive it. Her sister was the only thing in this hard, terrifying existence that was worth anything at all.

Finally, she reached the top. Climbing onto the thin metal rail, she stretched her arms up and wrapped her fingers along the edge of the roof. It had been easier when the three of them were together. She would boost Meredith up first, then Meredith would pull Sam up, and then the two of them would work together to pull Robyn up. Supporting her own weight entirely by her arms was much more challenging.

As she clambered onto the roof, a wave of relief washed over her, followed by an acute sense of fury. Meredith and Sam were lying in the sun together, Sam's head comfortably resting on her hands. Meredith was holding one of their novels up in front of them. She'd obviously been reading to Sam but she glanced over at the sound of Robin's footsteps.

"So, you decided to join the land of the living," Meredith said, then turned her attention back to the book.

"What are you doing up here? And how did you …" Robyn said.

"You were sleeping and Sam was bored. Nate offered to give us a boost."

Nate. "Don't you realize what he's doing? The only reason he's here is because he wants to use us. He's one of *them.*" That alone should have been enough for them.

"So what?" Sam said. "He wants to help us. He even gave you someone to help you be an Independent."

"He's not doing that out of the goodness of his heart."

Meredith shot a warning glance at her. She ignored it.

"He's using us," Robyn said. "He's not your friend."

"At least he's doing something," Sam said, sitting up. "All you do is tell us to stay inside, be quiet, keep the candle off. I've never even been to the market! And the only time you let us up here is when *you* feel like it." Her eyes were welling, and she angrily brushed a stray tear away. "Me and Meredith spent the morning dancing. And singing, Robyn. We were singing! Out loud! And we didn't care if anyone heard us."

"You should have," Robyn said. "So he taught you a game of cards. Helped you get up here. Told you it was safe to make noise. None of that changes the real world." She looked at Meredith. "You should know better. You're going to get her killed."

Her words must've struck home because Meredith's eyes narrowed. Meredith had already closed the book, and now she put her arm around Sam.

"There was nobody around," Meredith said. "I never would have endangered her. The girl's got to have a little bit of fun. She's six."

"That doesn't mean anything," Robyn said, fighting for control. "Not anymore."

"Then why do you treat me like it does? Like I'm little?" Sam whispered, tears finally streaming down her face. "And why do you have to ruin everything? I don't want to be scared all the time!"

Robyn worked to control her emotions. Her instinct was to get down on her knees with Sam and pull her close, to tell her she didn't have to be afraid. She wanted to believe Trevor's version of the future, one where she could actually have some sort of hope. Instead, she steadied herself against her own weakness and focused on reality. Sam needed to understand the way things were right now, not how they might be later.

Robyn turned away from them and looked out from the building. Meredith spoke something soothing and indistinguishable to Sam. Sam quieted and stilled. Robyn heard them settle in again, lying down on the concrete roof. There would be no more singing while she was there. They would be quiet and, most of all, they'd be safe. After a few moments, Meredith's voice began, gently reading. Robyn stared down at the streets below. Looking at the fire escape, she pictured Nate walking up here with them with his damaged hand and uneven gait. He would have had to be incredibly determined—stubborn, even—to make it all the way up and help an old woman and a small child onto the roof. Add to that the challenge of getting back down on his own. His iron will was obvious and, despite his physical limitations, he wasn't weak.

He had the kind of look she might have found appealing back home—or at least interesting. He was too skinny, of course, but the unusual color of his eyes paired with his sharp features had something that drew her gaze to his face. Not that she found him even remotely attractive. She pictured the way his smile never reached his cold eyes, the way he spoke to people as if what they wanted didn't matter at all, the way every sentence felt like a threat. He probably thought he could control her, like he had some sort of power. She wouldn't let him jeopardize her family, neither him nor Trevor. After all, Trevor was only working with her to benefit Nate. He might see himself as a kinder person than Nate, but everyone was the same: looking out for themselves or the people they cared about. Not that she blamed them. She was describing herself, too.

She knew it would be better for her family if she'd never met Nate or Trevor. If she'd never found the bike. Somehow, though, she couldn't bring herself to wish she could undo it.

CHAPTER 7

"What's the story with you and Robyn?" Trevor asked, letting himself into Nate's apartment.

Nate, leaning against the counter, looked up from the tin of corn he was working on. "It's broad daylight, Man. What are you doing here?"

"Bike's stashed. Nobody saw me come in. Plus, nobody knows I'm an Independent."

"But if they catch you," Nate said through a mouthful of kernels, "I don't want anybody thinking they saw us together."

Trevor shrugged. "Like I said, nobody saw me. Plus, I won't get caught."

"Whatever." Nate grabbed a second tin and tossed it across the room to Trevor. Since he and Robyn had been working, Nate had more than enough food. He'd been right about her. She was good on a bike, and she had a quick mind and enough to lose to make her willing to pay him his cut.

Trevor read the label as he joined Nate at the counter. "Beans?"

"You're welcome." He handed Trevor a knife.

"Thanks," Trevor said. The can popped as the knife pierced its side. "You didn't answer my question."

Nate watched him work the blade. "There is no story."

"Really? It's been over a week now and Robyn says, every time she comes back, you're there with her family. All week now."

"Robyn says what?" Nate raised an eyebrow. "I think the better question is, why do *you* care?"

"I don't." Trevor's voice was guarded. "Not if you do, you know?"

Nate laughed. "Of course." He wasn't surprised that Trevor was interested in this girl—or that he didn't want to move in on her if Nate were interested. If Trevor was anything, he was loyal. "Listen, I appreciate the offer, but I'm just keeping them close to remind her who's in charge. You're welcome to *enjoy* her company any way you want."

"You know that's not what I meant. And you're sure?"

"First off, I told you, I'm just keeping them close. Second, you realize she can't stand me, right? Not that I'm complaining, but she'd stab me in the back if she had the opportunity."

"She's warming up to you." Trevor didn't meet his eyes.

"Right."

"Or she will, anyway. I keep telling her you're not such a bad guy, deep down."

Ah. They'd been talking about him. He didn't need Trevor defending him. Besides, Trevor was wrong. There was nothing good inside of him. Robyn had seen it from the start. And every moment he spent with her family, working his way into their good opinion, confirmed it to her. She was smart enough to know he was using them to manipulate her, smart enough to know she had no choice but to let him.

"Don't do me any favors," Nate said. "Trust me, not

interested. Feel free."

"Hm." Trevor eyed him before settling back against the counter. Trevor scraped out the last of the food in the can and licked some off his fingers. "If you say so." He placed the empty tin back on the counter. "I have another reason for coming by, though."

"Oh, you're not risking our lives for a chat about girls, then?"

"Not *just* for a chat about girls. I actually also wanted to ask you if know about anyone who might be … friendly … to Independents in other neighborhoods, ones outside of Grim territory."

"You want to know? Or John Ashwood wants to? Because, last time I checked, I already found you a few places. Either you're getting greedy or you're asking for someone else."

"Okay, Coop." He held up his palms. "Yeah, it's for John. He has a few more Independents who came to him for help. He's trying to find them places to work."

"Right."

"He is. He's trying to help."

"And you're telling me he doesn't take a cut? He's doing this out of the goodness of his heart?"

"He doesn't take anything for his work. He feels called."

"I can't believe you're still buying that." Nate shook his head. "If Ashwood really cared about anyone besides himself, he'd tell you guys to give your bikes up and step in line. Doing what you're doing is just going to get you killed."

"Right. And working for the Grims always turned out so well for you."

"I'm better off than most people in the city." As soon as he'd said it, he knew Trevor would win this one.

"Exactly. That's *why* John is trying to help—because nobody's going to make it through whatever this is if we just let the gangs run things. I don't think anyone's coming to rescue us. We have to—" He stopped at the sound of wheels on pavement. They waited for the bikes to pass but, instead, they slowed outside Nate's place. Trevor started towards the back room.

"No time," Nate said as the footfalls sounded up the stairs outside. "You're just a source." The door swung open and Rob, his bike slung over his shoulder, walked in.

"Please, come in," Nate said dryly.

"Marshall wants to see you," Rob said. His eyes darted to Trevor, then back to Nate. "Who's that?"

"Source," Nate said, at the same time Trevor said, "Trevor."

"Trev's a source," Nate said. "Keeps an eye out for Independents trying to ride in our territory."

"Been more of that lately," Rob said. "But not for long." He looked at Trevor again. "Have anything good for us?"

"Nothing right now." Trevor studied the floor.

Nate needed to change the focus, fast. Trevor was a bad liar.

"What does Marshall need me for?" Nate asked. At Rob's shrug, he added, "Guess I won't keep him waiting, then." He waited for Trevor to leave, then Nate followed Rob out.

On the street, straddling a twenty-niner, was one of Marshall's lieutenants. His broad shoulders and over-muscled arms looked out of place, even on the larger bike. He lifted his chin towards Rob. "No problems?"

Rob shook his head. Nate grinned. "Come on, Berg. Thought this was just a friendly visit. What type of problems were you expecting?"

Berg smiled back, eyes glinting. "I guess I can only hope, right?"

Nate drew in a steady breath. He kept his face blank. Berg was the kind of guy who got off on hurting people weaker than he was, which was pretty much everyone. The fact that Marshall sent him along was a bad sign.

"How about I meet you guys there." Nate turned to his escorts after Trevor had disappeared safely down a side street. "You can get there a lot quicker than I can. Wouldn't want to waste everyone's day."

"We're supposed to make sure you make it okay." Rob's face was unreadable, but Berg was still grinning.

"He's the boss," Nate said, shrugging. "Let's go."

***

The gray concrete building loomed up ahead, the light from the midday sun reflecting off the glass doors at the front. Police had installed bulletproof glass the year before the blackout. The gang hadn't appreciated it back then but now it was one of the perks of being in Grim territory. The fires had destroyed most of the nearby buildings, but they'd worked hard to keep this one safe. It had paid off, too.

Nate ignored the sharp pain shooting from his knee into his thigh and hip and concentrated on keeping his face expressionless. Rob and Berg flanked him, walking their bikes. Neither men would say why Marshall wanted to see him, which meant either they didn't know themselves, or they knew Nate wouldn't like it. Nate could take a guess. It had to have something to do with Owen's death. If Jared and Rob were still wondering if he had anything to do with Owen's death, there was a good chance Marshall was, too.

As they neared the entrance, Rob shouted a greeting to the four armed Grims who stood outside the door. Two more would be guarding the side entrance and two at the back, by the attached multistorey parking garage. Getting control of River Ridge's central police station had been big in wrestling the power away from the cops. Once they had the station and the firearms inside, there wasn't really anything anyone could do. Fools kept waiting for the military to sweep in and save them, but nobody had come. He'd chosen the right side.

"You good for the stairs?" Rob asked from his left. "You're limping pretty bad."

Nate shot him a cold look. "I'm always limping pretty bad. It's how I walk now." It was partially true. But he knew his limp became more pronounced when he'd been walking for a distance. He hated Rob for saying it. "I'm fine."

His escorts stopped at the foot of the long, wide stairway leading up from the front entrance. Nate forced himself forward. Clearly, he was supposed to go in alone. The banister was still intact, and he grasped it firmly, using it to steady himself and take some weight off the bad leg. It was worse that there were witnesses. He tried not to think of Rob's eyes following him as he awkwardly limped up the stairs. The reinforced panes of the once-automatic glass doors reflected his own face back at him. A bead of sweat trickled down his temple, despite the cool fall air, and his brow was furrowed in concentration and pain. He forced the image away as he slid the heavy doors open. He managed to do it in a single, smooth motion that almost made up for the humiliation of his slow ascent up the stairs.

He stepped inside, leaving the others behind him on the sidewalk. He'd been here plenty of times before the blackout—arrested as a juvie and released—but more times later on. He'd enjoyed the irony when he locked up his first cop.

"Nate!" Marshall Ward's big voice echoed through the main foyer as he approached. Marshall was smiling at him, which should have been a relief, but Marshall was one of those men whose smile never quite reached his eyes.

Nate forced his own expression into what he hoped resembled a relaxed smile as the larger man reached him.

"What can I do for you?" Nate asked, extending his hand.

Marshall grasped it, then gestured for Nate to follow. "Come with me."

Nate struggled to keep up with Marshall's pace. Nate appreciated it though. Marshall never treated him like a person with a handicap. Of course, that could be because Marshall didn't lower his expectations for anyone.

They strode down the long narrow corridor that led farther into the station. It was dark in the hallways, but the thin, slatted windows near the high ceilings let in enough light. At night, the candles they'd attached along the upper edges of the wall would be lit.

What did Marshall want with him? "Hey, Marshall," he called as they turned off down another hallway. He knew exactly where they were. They were nearing the hall that led to the holding cells. They did the majority of interrogations there. People often didn't last the night. "Sorry about what happened with Owen." He tried to keep his voice steady, light. "I did everything I could for him. I hope you believe that."

Marshall dismissively waved his hand and continued down the hallway. "Owen allowed himself to get stuck by an Independent. His death is on his own head." In other words, it seemed he didn't care if Nate had killed him or not. Nate was in the clear for that. So why was he here?

They turned again and then stopped at the inner conference room. This was where Marshall gathered the crew for planning and reviewing strategies. Before Marshall opened the door, Nate knew it would be just the two of them. Since his injury, Nate didn't get to go to those meetings. Instead, he met with Marshall alone to go over his intel and to use his nearly photographic memory to plan the routes for him. But Nate wasn't due for a re-route meeting for at least another month. Marshall pushed open the heavy door and Nate hurried to catch it before it shut on him. Nate glanced up at the large, pull-down screen once used for projected images. The map of River Ridge they'd taken from City Hall before it had burned to the ground was still tacked up there, thick red lines marking the Grims' territory. The neighborhoods that had burned to ashes were crossed out, and the abandoned areas, the ones that were unlivable, were grayed out in pencil, including the one in which Trevor was working with Robyn.

"Routes I laid out still good?" Nate asked, trying for casual.

"Sure. No problems. Grims have them solid."

Nate waited beside him as Marshall traced his finger along the routes Nate had penciled in for him less than a month ago.

"Routes are great. But the problem we're having is that, somehow, they're not keeping the Independents at bay. Owen, for example. It was his own fault, but the Independents should never have been here. And there was that other Independent we shot, the one whose bike just disappeared before our crew could get it. Other sightings too. Somehow, they're slipping through." Nate caught his sidelong glance. "Any ideas how that's happening?"

Nate kept his face carefully blank. "No idea." He silently reminded himself he was telling the truth. He hadn't done anything to help those Independents. He'd only given Trevor a route and used the girl who'd taken the bike for her own. That didn't make him guilty, did it? But it wouldn't matter to Marshall how he'd helped the Independents, just that he had.

"You haven't heard anything? Listening's your specialty. It's one of the things we keep you around for."

Was that a threat? "Nothing. But I'll ask around."

"Do that." Marshall shook his head. "If we could catch Ashwood, we could stop this infestation. He's training more of them every day."

"I'll keep my ears open. I'll find him."

"I hope so." Marshall turned away. "Thanks for stopping by."

That was it? He'd walked for nearly an hour and a half through their territory to meet Marshall here. There was no way that was all the guy wanted. Nate followed him back through the halls. They slowed as they neared the holding cells.

Marshall stopped at the doorway. "Just need to make a quick stop in to see Jared. Join me."

Not a request.

Nate followed Marshall through the door and down a set of narrow stairs into a basement room. The small, familiar room was lit with candles, and the two Members sitting at the table glanced up as they entered. He'd had this duty before, when he was whole. Guarding the holding cells. It was unnecessary—the locks still functioned on keys. They didn't need electricity to keep their prisoners secure; it wasn't as if they'd need to keep them for long. Most people they locked up never walked out.

"Hey, Marshall." The kid closest to the stairs stood quickly. He was young, barely an adolescent. They must be recruiting. "He's still in there with Alan."

Alan? Nate and Alan had joined the Grims at the same time. He hadn't seen Alan since before the accident. What were Jared and Alan doing in the cell?

Marshall nodded and the boy sat.

"Jared!" Marshall called out as they entered the small area in front of the cells. "Any luck?"

Nate swallowed the bile that rose in his throat. The smell was almost overpowering. Jared rose from a crouched position over Alan. Blood pooled around the body. As Jared turned to face them, Nate forced his eyes to Jared's. Jared grinned. Unlike his father, Jared's face was easy to read: he enjoyed his work.

"Not much. He admitted he was a traitor. Was really sorry about it, too." Jared laughed, shaking his head. "As if we wouldn't have caught him."

"That's it?" Marshall asked.

"Gave up the names of some of the Independents. Some streets they work. But nothing new."

Marshall toed Alan's shoulder. "Wish you'd kept him alive. Hangings are good reminders."

"We can put him out like this."

"It'll have to do." Marshall fixed a steady gaze on Nate. "It's a real blow when the people you trust betray you."

"No kidding," Nate said, returning the look.

"Keep your ears open. Counting on you." Marshall turned back to his son, clapping him on the shoulder.

Nate was dismissed. He turned and made his way past the kids in the entrance and back up the stairs, away from the smell and the body and the people he used to consider family.

He walked as quickly as his leg would let him. This whole thing was set up as a warning. Marshall suspected him. This was supposed to scare him into confessing. Or messing up. He knew it.

But what was he supposed to do about it? He already had the girl working. He could turn her in, but what would stop her from telling the Grims about his part? He could kill her himself, say he was tipped off, bring them back the bike.

He pictured Robyn's face. Somehow, he couldn't see himself doing it. It wasn't like he cared about her or her family. It was just… He shook the thought away before he could finish it. Personal feelings aside, he liked the arrangement they had. It had been working well for him. He was turning a profit, getting his hands on more tradable goods than the Grims were willing to give him. Plus, he had a feeling that, if he got rid of Robyn, Trevor would never forgive him. Nate wasn't sure why, but somehow he didn't think he could live with that.

"Back already?" Rob sounded surprised as Nate exited the station. Berg was already gone.

Nate nodded, squinting into the light. This threat, or warning—or whatever this was—would end up costing him his entire day with the walk back. But if Marshall had any real proof—if he knew Nate was dirty for sure—there was no way he'd be walking out of here at all. No. All they had were suspicions and Jared's accusations. Nothing concrete. He'd just have to watch his back more closely and make sure Robyn and Trevor did the same.

CHAPTER 8

It was drizzling by the time Robyn and Trevor made their way back through the park, riding slowly side-by-side. Her skills and stamina had improved in the last two weeks. She knew this would be their last night together. Tomorrow, she'd be solo.

Meredith and Sam would have put the buckets out to collect the water. Rain was always a good thing.

"We're lucky it's just rain," Trevor said, breaking the silence of the still night. "In a few weeks, we could have snow. Then it's a whole new game."

"Do you have a fatbike?" she asked. She'd seen some Members riding them last winter: large bikes with oversized wheels. With their big, wide tires, they were never hung up in the snow, and pretty much no terrain was off limits. Back home in California, some riders used them for sand dune riding. She'd never really seen the draw until she'd seen them used in the Canadian winter.

"Nah. I'll just chain my tires. That usually does the trick. Worked last winter."

"Bet you made a killing in the winter. We traded most of

our food last year for gloves and jackets." She shook her head. "Then, this summer, we traded those out for food."

"I'll keep my eyes open for some warm gear for you guys," he said. "And, yeah, it's true that people get desperate in the winter, but you lose a lot of customers, too."

He didn't have to explain. People froze in the winter, not only on the streets but also in their homes. And the danger wasn't just from the cold. People died trying to keep warm—fires or carbon monoxide poisoning or smoke inhalation.

Robyn wondered what things were like back home. Did they have power yet? Was their government functioning? Were they going to send help?

"I'll also stop in some time after the winter hits and help you prep your bike," he added, glancing over at her. She could just barely make him out now.

"Sure." She kept her voice low as they approached the narrow passageway.

They paused in front of it. They would fall silent as they made their way through and then part as usual.

"It's been fun having some company," he said. "Usually being an Independent is kind of ..."

"Independent?" she said, smiling.

"I was going to say lonely, but yeah."

She wished she could see his face. His pedal clinked as he positioned his foot.

"Well, you know, now that this is *my* route, you can always tag along some time. When you're bored with your greener pasture and all."

"Maybe I'll do that," he said. Then he pushed off. "See you around." He disappeared into the darkness.

Robyn waited a moment before following and, when she

came out the other side, he was gone.

As she pedaled along the familiar route home, her backpack weighed on her shoulders. The rain picked up, and soon she was riding blind. She slowed, concentrating on not sliding out in the slick grit under her tires and on staying tucked in tight to the wall. Finally, she saw the tiny light from her basement up ahead. Of course she saw the light. Nate was with them, and he seemed to think they were invisible. She never would have allowed a lighted candle in the pitch black. Even though part of her knew it was a tiny light, and she was probably only aware of it because she was looking for it, she couldn't help but feel like it was a giant beacon announcing their location to every predatory creep and Grim out there.

Inside, she wasn't surprised to see Nate sitting at the table. Sam and Meredith were sleeping in the bed, which was already pulled away from the wall to allow her to put the bike away without waking them.

Nate's arms were crossed on the table surface in front of him and his head was turned sideways, resting on his forearms. His eyes were closed.

Some protector.

She was dripping and chilled, but she didn't want to change with him in the room. She had spare khakis, dull brown with both knees torn and the hem far too long for her, folded up and shoved into the shelf along with her bright orange T-shirt. They would be dry and warm. *Maybe the next room?*

Nate shifted slightly, and the reality of him waking up and coming to look for her was sobering enough to stay wet.

He insisted on coming over every night right before she left. She didn't like it, but Meredith, she knew, was no fool when it came to protecting Samantha. Meredith claimed they felt safer when he was there and believed he really would protect them if something happened while Robyn was out. Even so, Meredith still watched him like a hawk. Mostly, according to Sam and Meredith, he just hung out with them for a while before they turned in for the night, and then he "kept watch." Yeah, if keeping watch entailed eating their food and reading their books.

And sleeping.

She couldn't stand the way he was working his way into their lives. She knew he just wanted to make sure he had his leverage and he got his cut when she returned. After stashing her bike, she placed the bag on the table across from him. He was completely out.

She studied his face in the flickering light. He had a thin scar she hadn't noticed before; it began just left of his right eyebrow and curved down almost parallel to his ear, stopping at his jaw line. It wasn't disfiguring exactly, although she imagined at some point it had been. It was obviously an old injury, maybe from before the blackout? She supposed violence was part of his everyday life after he joined the Grims. At fifteen, no less. On her fifteenth birthday, she'd raced in the qualifiers for the Jr. Riders' Competitive League. She'd come in second out of seventy racers.

She looked away. Opening her pack, she drew out her take: two tins of some kind of fish, a can of corn, three candles, and a book by Dr. Seuss. The house she'd gotten the book from had been little more than half a small shack. Trevor had sent her up the walk alone and, when the woman inside came to the door, Robyn had been struck by her hollow, gaunt cheeks and the deep lines under her eyes. She looked more like a skeleton than a human being. Like many others, she wanted to trade for matches. She was lucky; Robyn had just picked some up at the last place.

"I don't have anything to pay you with," the woman said, her voice shaking.

Robyn had a moment of indecision. She couldn't just give things away. Trevor was clear on the importance of maintaining strict business relationships, although she'd seen him bend his own rules more than once. She steadied herself. She had to look out for her family. If word got out she was giving things away …

"Would you take a children's book?" the woman said. "My little girl passed last month. Maybe someone else could use it …"

Robyn knew she got the better end of the deal, even though books were more or less useless on the market. People were looking to survive; she'd discovered that when she'd tried to hock Meri's books. She was relieved nobody had taken them. They were nearly the only good thing left in Sam's life.

Now, Robyn took the book and the corn and returned them to the bag. If Nate saw the book, he would haggle with her over it, to get more of the food from her. Later, when he was gone, she'd fish it out and put it with her own supplies. She would like to have taken more, but he'd know.

Zipping the pack securely, she crossed the room as silently as she could and shoved the bag under the bed. She'd have to wake him sooner or later. Barely breathing, she fingered the switchblade she'd started carrying in her pocket.

How hard would it be to …? But she couldn't even finish the thought. She might have let the cyclist die, but she wasn't a murderer. At least, not yet.

His eyes flew open and she found herself looking directly into them. He abruptly sat up. "Thinking of strangling me in my sleep?" he asked, his hoarse voice strangely at odds with his light tone.

"Something like that," she murmured, quickly walking to the goods she'd left on the table.

"That's all?" He eyed her closely.

"It's getting cold. People are trying to save what they have for winter."

He muttered something unintelligible, but he didn't press her.

"Here," she said, pushing a candle and a tin over to him.

"Why do you get two candles?" His stupid grin was back.

"I think it's only fair since you insist on using ours up every night." She swept the candles and the tin into her hands and put them into the cupboards. Since she'd started as an Independent, and since they'd had Nate with them, she'd begun keeping food on the shelves. It was nice to actually have something to store. "Especially when you're just sleeping anyway. What, you afraid of the dark now?"

"Ha ha." His smile faded. "I was bored. You need some more books or something. Put that on your little list."

"You know, I still can't believe you can read," she said, rolling her eyes.

"Whatever." He got awkwardly to his feet, shoving the can in one pocket and the candle in the other. He paused, frowning. "You're soaked."

"I noticed, thanks."

"You're going to get sick. You can't stay wet like that." He'd turned towards her.

She took a step back. "Again, thanks. I'm waiting until you're gone."

"Why?" He snorted, then seemed to realize her hesitation. "Oh, come on. I'm not some kind of desperate animal who jumps at—" He stopped suddenly.

"Really?"

"Shhh." He put his fingers to his lips and leaned back

slightly, listening.

She strained to hear. There was a slight rustling of leaves from the wind and the steady patter of rain. What could he possibly—

"Go," he whispered and, without a second thought, she sprinted across the room to Meredith and Sam.

Before she even reached the bed, the window flung open. Sam screamed at the sudden noise. Nate fumbled with the gun in his belt, but it slipped from his grasp and clattered to the floor.

"Take her," Robyn said to Meredith, who was already on her feet, pulling Sam up.

It was too late.

A man jumped down from the window. Nate threw himself at him, using his body weight to pin him down. He started punching him with his good arm. Meredith held Sam's trembling hand and pulled her through the hole in the wall. Covering the hole was pointless now. Robyn had left it wide open when she'd parked the bike.

"Come on!" Meredith shouted.

"Just take her!" Maybe Robyn could buy them some time. A second man landed in the small room. "Now!"

"No. We can't ..." With a sob, Sam yanked her hand from Meredith's firm grip and ran towards Robyn.

The second man, seeing the child running through the small room, grabbed her around her waist and lifted her off the ground. She thrashed around screaming, and Meredith rushed towards them. She didn't seem to notice the small pistol in his hand—or didn't care, maybe—but the bang was deafening as the man dropped Sam and fired. Meredith slumped to the ground. Sam's mouth opened in a scream as she ran to Meredith, but all Robyn could hear was a horrible ringing. She stared at the shooter, who had aimed the gun at her and was trying to fire again. She couldn't make herself move. Everything was happening so fast. Her legs wouldn't work; her feet were somehow pinned to the floor. Her heart raced. *What just happened?*

The man threw the gun down and lunged towards her, but then he suddenly stopped. His body jerked and his eyes opened wide in surprise. Or pain, maybe. He turned towards Nate, who was now standing. Robyn could see a long, thin knife handle protruding from her attacker's upper back, between his shoulder blades. Nate had stabbed him.

Nate didn't give him a chance to recover. He leapt at the intruder, falling down on top of him, his one strong hand wrapped around his throat.

The world came back into sharp focus.

Sobbing. Loud gut-wrenching sobs blended with the quick gasps of the dying man beneath Nate's iron grasp. Finally looking away, Robyn crossed the small space to kneel down beside her sister.

Sam desperately clutched Meredith's limp hand. Meredith's eyes were open, fixed on some unseen point beyond them.

"I told her not to go." Sam's words came out in a breathless rush. "She just touched my face, and then …"

"Shh," Robyn tried, but Sam wasn't listening.

"And then she just left. Just like Mom and Dad. Now I have no one."

"Shhh," Robyn said again. "You have me."

"I have no one," she said again, draping her body over Meredith's.

Robyn heard Nate get up behind her. There was no other noise and no real sense of urgency in his uneven gate. He breathed heavily. He'd saved them. She knew he had—and yet she was horrified by the brutality she'd seen in his face as he struggled with the man.

"We need to go." Nate's voice was quiet and steady.

Sam didn't even look up. Robyn, though, glanced around. The candle had almost burnt itself out now, but the sky was starting to lighten and the rain had let up.

"Are they …" Robyn said.

"They're dead. But we need to get out of here before more come."

"How do you know there'll be more?"

"Look." He gestured to the men. They wore red bandanas. Part of his crew. "They wouldn't have come out here in the middle of the night with just two unless they'd been watching you. Unless they knew you had something they wanted."

Like my bike, Robyn thought.

"And if these two knew you were here, other people in the Grims know, too. Nobody goes anywhere without permission." He was quiet for a moment, then added, "And that's Jared Ward" —he motioned to the second attacker, the one who'd killed Meredith—"Marshall's kid."

CHAPTER 9

The silence in the room was crushing. Nate waited as Robyn absorbed the revelation of who Jared was. Everyone knew Marshall Ward led the Grims—if his son were dead, he'd be out for blood.

"And you knew them? Personally?" Robyn asked, her voice hollow.

Maybe she found it strange the attackers had names. Names and families. He forced the thought away. He had no love for Rob and Jared—but they were Grims. They were part of his crew.

He nodded. "'Course. I didn't realize it at first but, after I saw Rob's face" —he gestured to Rob— "I knew. He and Jared were partners."

"What now?" she asked.

"I guess we go. Soon, before it gets too light out. Sun's rising. You can come to my place but you can't stay long. Just until we can figure out what to do. And you need to get changed."

She was still soaking, and Sam's jeans were covered in Meredith's blood. Robyn got to her feet. As she stuffed clothes and supplies into the two empty backpacks and a third one from the floor, Nate picked up his 9mm from the ground and shoved it back into his waistband. If he hadn't dropped it, maybe he could have stopped them before …

"Come on," Nate said to Sam, touching her shoulder. She jerked her body away. "We need to go." He grabbed her by the wrist.

She looked up at him, her eyes wild and unfocused. "They killed her!" she screeched, the high-pitched, frantic sound cracking on the last word. Then she fell on top of Meredith again, tiny sobs shaking her shoulders.

Robyn moved towards her sister, but Nate, already there, hauled the little girl to her feet.

"And we're next if we don't get out of here," he said, looking at Sam. She tried to pull away but his grip held firm. "When these guys don't get back to the station, more men will come looking for them, and they will have guns. And if they find us here, we end like her." He nodded toward Meredith. "Or worse."

Something in his tone drove the resistance out of Samantha, and she stopped pulling away from him. He let her go, and she ran past him to Robyn and hugged her waist.

"You have an exit through there?" He gestured to the hole in the wall.

"Yeah," Robyn said, "but what do we do with the bike?"

"We bring it," he said. "I'll walk it to my place. The sun's on its way up. It's light enough out there for people to be able to tell I'm wearing colors. Nobody will think it's weird for a Member to have a bike. I mean, unless they think too carefully about what a cripple is doing with a bicycle. But, if anyone asks, I'm bringing it for the Grims."

"How do I know you're not?" Robyn asked.

"I could have killed you and taken your bike a long time

ago. Better yet, I could have let them." She didn't have to turn around to know who he was talking about. "Now give me some paper. I'll draw you a map to my place."

She handed him the small, folded paper she'd been using to record goods, along with the small pencil she carried. He drew the map on top of it. He handed it back, then grabbed the bike.

"Careful," he said, "and be quick."

They went through the hole and out the other room's exit into a blackened hallway. With no windows, there was really no way to see what direction they were going, but they ran their fingers along the wall until they got to the back staircase.

"You need help getting the bike up?" she asked.

He simply grunted. He didn't need her pity. The dim light from dawn filtered in as he pulled the bike up from the dark and onto the street.

"Give me a minute to get out of here," he said, "but don't wait too long." He let the door shut behind him.

The sky was pink and golden now, as the sun rose over the horizon. Nobody would even notice it, or care now, if they did. Most of the apartment suites within had collapsed or had been completely flooded, and hers was not much better.

But it was home for them.

They could never go back. Sam had been trembling when he'd left. He forced himself to feel nothing. Pity wouldn't help. He needed to be cold and clear-headed. Still, the sound of her sobs echoed in his ears.

He neared his apartment. Robyn and Sam would follow soon enough. His map was perfect, and his apartment door, marked with the red X to signify a Grim residence, would be easy to see from a distance.

Inside, he leaned against the far wall, watching the door,

anxious. If the Grims caught Robyn and Sam, he had no doubt they'd turn him in. He would, if the roles were reversed.

Come on. Come on.

She didn't knock.

"It's about time," he said as she came through, holding Sam's hand.

She pushed the door closed hard behind her. Her eyes quickly swept the area, no doubt taking in the small square coffee table with its low footstool and the single shelving unit that took up the opposite wall. She seemed surprised. Had she assumed it would be better furnished, considering his membership? It used to be.

"Emptier than you thought, right?" He shrugged. "It's not bad though." He nodded to his right and she looked past him to the doorway. He knew she'd see his small, single bed against the back wall. "Anyway, that's why I needed you working for me. When you can't ride, you can't collect. Life becomes more minimalist."

Robyn pulled Sam closer. "So what's the next move?"

The next move? He had no idea. They were just lucky the Grims didn't have guys stationed at his house yet. Maybe they didn't know he was involved. Robyn and Sam looked at him, waiting, trusting him to have some sort of answer.

"You brought clothes?" he asked, gesturing to her pack. At her nod, he said, "You two get changed. There's some water stored in a bucket in there. You can use a little to … clean up. I guess you hide out here until I can contact Trev. He knows someone who can help." Even as he said it, he hated himself. John Ashwood was pretty much their only option now.

She nodded and led Sam into his room, closing the door behind her. It felt strange, staring at the closed door. He didn't think it had been shut since he'd moved in here.

When they came out again, Samantha, still ashen and listless, was in dry jeans and a small hoodie. Robyn, though, was in torn brown Khakis and an orange T-shirt. Not subtle by any means. And not warm enough for the weather.

"You can't wear that," he said. She raised her eyebrows at him. "You'll freeze."

"My pullover is wet and it was my only one."

"Here." He limped over to his cupboard. In the lower shelves, beneath the food, were his extra sweaters. Not that anything would fit her. He'd always been skinny, and it was worse since the blackout. Robyn was pretty thin, too, but he was broad and tall; she would drown in his clothes. He pulled out the smallest black hooded sweatshirt he could find. "Put it on." He tossed it to her.

She caught it. "No, thanks."

"Seriously," he said. "You're already shivering."

She looked down at the shirt in her hand, then pulled it on. It was, of course, far too big, hanging down mid-thigh. She rolled the sleeves up over her wrist.

"It's fleece inside," she said, and he could already see her shivering subsiding. "Thanks."

He glanced away from her. "Yeah, well, you're going to need to be functional if you want to get out of here." Samantha stood in the middle of the room, staring at the wall. "She okay?"

"I think so." She followed his gaze, staring at her sister. "Sam," she finally said, "Meri's in a better place."

Sam's eyes glanced to Robyn's face. "You don't believe that."

"Meri did."

Sam whispered something so quietly Nate was sure Robyn didn't hear her either.

"What'd you say, Kid?" Nate asked.

Samantha met his eyes. "I said it was my fault," she said, her voice little more than a whisper.

"Why would you say that?"

"She was coming back into the room to get me. If I'd just listened …"

The kid blames herself.

Robyn's mouth opened to reply, but Nate interrupted. "Sam," he said, "the only people who were responsible for Meredith's death were the guys who came into your home. Not you. Not anyone else."

He was surprised at the emotion that suddenly choked him. Maybe it was habit, pretending to care about them? Maybe, he admitted, it was also that it wasn't fair. Why should she have to shoulder the guilt of that woman's death? Meredith had died doing what she lived for: keeping Samantha safe. For some reason, that counted for something. It had to.

"And if Meredith believed she'd be in a better place, you gotta respect that, right?" he said.

Sam nodded slowly. "I guess."

He cleared his throat, embarrassed by Robyn's stare. "Get some sleep, Kiddo. You're safe; your sister's safe. Meri would want that."

"I'll tuck you in," Robyn said to her sister. She took Sam's hand and led her into Nate's room.

He moved again to the window. People were stirring now. As long as nobody suspected him yet, the girls could hide out here until nightfall. If the Grims had known about him, they would have been waiting here, or they would have shown up by now. He stared at his closed door. Almost without thinking, he touched the butt of the 9mm tucked into his jeans. As long as nobody had seen them together, he was in the clear. Or would be without the two loose ends in his room. Loose ends. The answer was simple, really. He'd protected them in the heat of things without thinking. But now he was clear-headed. Now …

Robyn emerged from the room. "She's sleeping." She eased the door shut. "Your bed's like a rock, but I don't think she noticed; she was so tired."

In the early light filtering in through the window, Robyn looked pretty exhausted herself. Somehow, she seemed younger to him than before. Some of her hair had escaped her elastic, and long red-brown strands framed her face.

She attempted a smile, maybe the first one ever aimed at him. "Thanks, by the way."

He knew what the smart thing to do was. He should have done it after Marshall threatened him at the compound. But he hadn't done it then and he knew that, for whatever reason, he couldn't do it now. He was getting soft. He eased his fingers away from the gun and shoved his hand into his pocket instead.

"Do you believe Meredith's in a better place?" she asked.

He laughed. "I guess it wouldn't take much to be in a better place than this, but we're not six years old, and I don't know how anyone can look around at the city here" —he gestured to the window— "and believe in anything."

Robyn leaned her back against Sam's door. "I know. I just …"

Nate turned from the window to look at her. Her eyes were clouded with something like grief.

"Meredith really believed it," she said. "Even after everything she lost—her husband, her own kids. She had her happiness ripped away from her one person at a time and still …" Her voice broke. He took a step towards her.

"Coop!" The door swung open and a skinny kid in a thin T-shirt, frayed jeans, and a dirty red bandana burst in. "Jared's dead. Marshall—" He stopped as he saw Robyn standing there and the bike leaning against the wall.

"Eric," Nate started, but the kid disappeared back through the door. He could hear him through the open doorway shouting down the street. It was too late. "Take the bike." He shoved it at Robyn.

"I'm not leaving Sam."

"Take the bike. You gotta lead them away. Trevor told me how you are on that thing. If you want her to have a chance, you need to get them to follow you." He knew she didn't trust him, but it was the only way they would all make it out. "I'll keep her safe. I promise you." When she hesitated, he pushed it at her again. "Go. Now. I'll get her out, but you need to go. We'll meet you in the territory Trev's been working with you. In that park."

With a frustrated groan, she grabbed the handlebars from him, pulling the bike around.

"Get her out," she said. "If anything happens to her …"

He understood the threat but shook his head. "I'm a dead man if we're caught, thanks to you." He pulled his red bandana from his neck and tossed it to her. "You might need this later."

She caught it and shoved it into her pocket. She hopped on the bike and, leaning back in ready, flew down the stairs. As she pulled onto the cracked sidewalk, a gunshot shattered the air. It was close. Through the window, he watched Robyn duck, hop the curb, and glance up towards the approaching Grims. He knew she was counting on them giving chase.

Sure enough, they veered towards her. Picking up speed, she careened around the corner. She'd bought him minutes. Others would be coming for him.

"Sam!" he shouted, limping across the room in the closest thing he had to a run. He yanked open the door to find her already on her feet, running towards him. "We've gotta go."

"Where's Robyn?"

"She's going to meet us. Come on."

She took his hand without another word and ran with him to the front door.

The street was empty now; nobody wanted to be in the way when the Grims were hunting. She followed him into the side alley. The primary target would be the Independent. It would be Robyn. There were more shouts from the street. He forced himself to move, to pick up his pace, to ignore the pain shooting up his leg. They turned again, staying close to the walls. It would be only moments until the Grims discovered he was gone. Only moments until they started the search. Again, he turned. If he had something valuable to trade, something worth something, he might be able to buy his own way out of this situation. Bribe someone to let him past. But he had nothing. He needed to disappear, and as fast as possible.

He knew this neighborhood better than anyone. Every path, every alleyway. He knew, too, the search routes they'd use. He'd helped design them. He turned out onto the main street and then off again into another back street.

"Where are we going?" Sam asked, still keeping pace with him.

"Somewhere safe," he said.

"I'm getting all turned around."

"Hopefully the Grims are, too."

They were nearing the passageway to the burnt-out area. The Grims had it mapped, thanks to him, but it wouldn't be on their minds now. They'd think to search it eventually, when they had a chance to study the map he'd drawn them, but he'd have to hope he could wait for Trevor there. He had to hope they'd have some time. He wished he'd thought of a way to signal his friend.

They came out the end of the passageway. He hadn't been here since he'd studied the route for the gang. It seemed just as deserted as he remembered it. If he didn't know differently, he would believe the ruse that it was abandoned. Trevor was teaching these people well.

"Where now?" Sam asked.

He looked around. He had to find somewhere he'd be able to see Trevor as he rode past. He'd told Robyn to meet them at the park, but it wasn't central.

"Nate!" Sam screamed, her hold on his hand tightening. She pointed into the distance. A rider rapidly approached. He knew the stride. He knew the bike and rider.

"It's okay," he said, lightly squeezing Sam's hand. "It's Trevor."

Trevor slid to a stop in front of them. "Where's Robyn?" he asked, scanning the area behind them.

"Trying to buy us some time. She's on her bike, taking the Grims for a ride."

Trevor's frown deepened and he ran his hands through his hair. "How long ago was this?"

"No idea." Nate felt an unexpected flash of anger at the question. "She left just ahead of us. I told her to meet us at that park you love so much. She'll be there once she's lost them."

"You okay?" Trevor was talking to Sam. She moved closer to Nate.

"You remember Trev, right?" Nate said. "He works with your sister. He's my friend." He glanced back at Trevor. "And I'm fine, too. Thanks for asking."

Trevor clasped his shoulder. "Sorry. I didn't even know you were involved. One of our contacts sent word that the Grims found out an Independent was living in their territory with a kid and an old woman. I was on my way to warn them."

"You're too late."

"They killed Meredith," Sam said, her voice quiet but steady. "Nate saved us."

"Nate?"

"Don't look so surprised," Nate said. His chest tightened. "Anyway, I probably made it worse. Rob and Jared."

"Dead?"

"I didn't have a choice." He didn't tell him how he'd dropped his gun, how he'd had to use his hands, how he felt sick when he thought of Jared's lifeless face. "Afterwards, Robyn and Sam were hiding out at my place when the Grims stopped by to fill me in. Robyn led them away so Sam and I could escape."

"Robyn's always leaving," Sam said, scuffing her shoe against the concrete. "She didn't even say bye this time."

"I'm so sorry about your friend," Trevor said. "Robyn will be back. She's a good rider. If anyone can get away from them, she can."

He was right, but hearing Trevor talking to Sam—about Robyn—bothered Nate. Maybe it was because he knew, even after everything he'd lost helping them, he was no hero. Trevor was. Sam didn't see it yet, but she would. And Robyn had always known it. No matter how much Nate did, it would never be enough because he was still who he'd always been.

"Speaking of safe, I'd like to stay that way," Nate said. "We need to get out of the open here. If I remember, there's not much coverage at the park, but at least it's not in the middle of the street." He started forward, Sam instantly moving with him. Trevor rolled his bike alongside them. "We're going to need Ashwood's help," Nate added, his voice low.

Trevor nodded but, thankfully, didn't say anything.

Nate glanced down at Sam, who was still grasping his hand tightly, her expression serious. She must trust him completely. He knew she tried to be strong, like her sister. But she was a child, with a child's faith in him. The last person who'd trusted him—*really* trusted him—was his step-brother. And he'd failed him, just like he'd failed Sam and Robyn.

Robyn flew down the next road and then the one after that, snaking her way around the neighborhood while trying to stay in the streets she knew. One benefit of no electricity was there was no instant communication about her location, no roadblocks, no check stops. It didn't stop Members who saw the pursuit from joining in though. They might not have known the situation, but they would soon enough. For most of them, it was the thrill of the chase and the promise of swift retribution for whatever offence had been committed. And seeing a non-Member on a bike was reason enough, anyway.

The time she'd spent training with Trevor had strengthened her muscles and brought back the techniques she'd spent her adolescence honing. The Members, although they lived on bikes now, had no reason to push themselves like the Independents. No real training. She glanced back. The gap between them had widened.

She swung around the next corner, slowing only a little before picking up speed. The buildings beside her blurred; the noise of the wind and her heartbeat drowned out the sound of her tires eating up the pavement. A few more feet, and she'd have lost them. She glanced behind her. Nothing. She faced forward again. There were riders approaching in the distance, their red colors signaling Grim membership.

She reached the intersection before they did, and she banked a hard right. There was a large, heavy green dumpster ahead. She hoped nobody was inside. With the rain the night before, there was a good chance that, if someone had been living there, they'd have cleared out to find better shelter. Pulling her brakes, she jumped off the bike even while it was still moving and, grabbing the stem and frame, flung it up and over into the bin. Hoisting herself up and scrambling over the edge after it, she landed hard on her bike and then lay flat, facedown, on top of it. She wretched at the smell and clamped her hand over her mouth. Most of the rainwater had drained out the holes in the bottom, but there was a mass of damp paper beneath her, and spongy, wet materials someone had likely been using for a bed. So much for Nate's dry hoodie.

She heard the riders turn into the street at the same time something small and furry brushed against her ankle. *A rat.* She willed herself to lie still, even as sharp claws scurried up and over her leg. It wouldn't take much for the Members to find her, lying in the dumpster under the bright sunlight. The rat chewed on the hem of her pants. Shuddering, she fought the growing sense of panic threatening to overwhelm her. Rodents didn't used to freak her out like this but, when the power didn't come back on and the backup generators at the CDC eventually failed, the rats became carriers of some of the worst viruses out there. That, and they were just gross.

Finally, the bikes rattled past her green coffin and the voices faded in the distance. She waited as long as her body would let her, and then she pulled herself up, knocking the rat off into the bottom of the dumpster. She peered out at the street. There was nobody coming. She'd either been fast enough to convince them she'd lost them, or they were still riding the nearby streets looking for her. Whatever the case, she had to find Sam. She heaved her bike back over the edge. She was surprised at its weight. It had felt so light when she'd first thrown it in.

Robyn stood beside her bike and stared down the bright street. She'd be a target for every Member on this bike, not wearing any colors. She pulled out Nate's bandana and tied it around her head. *I'm a Grim. Grims don't move for anyone.* Her instinct was, of course, to ride along the edge of the lane near the buildings, but that wouldn't fool anyone. Grims owned the streets.

She set out again, this time forcing herself to stay centered, riding fast but not fast enough to draw attention to herself. Her hands were moist on her grips. Not many people had seen her and there wouldn't be any drawings circulating yet, but there'd be descriptions going around. They'd be talking about what she was wearing and what she looked like. And here she was, riding her bike in the center of the road in the middle of the day.

At one of the crossroads, two Members rode past. She was thankful they didn't look too closely. Each gang would know its Members, at least superficially.

How did Nate feel, having killed one of his own? Was Sam safe? What if it were a trick and his intention were to turn her in? The small knife still sat in her pocket. It wouldn't be much good against anybody with a real weapon, but it would be good for one thing if Sam was gone. Because how could she go on without her sister?

She neared the passageway and picked up speed. With a

quick glance around, she turned down the alley leading to the passageway and then, with another turn, she was there, passing through it.

She came out the other side into the bright sunlight again. She didn't see anyone. The streets were mostly empty.

She pushed down the street, then down another one and into the park. She stopped and caught her breath. There were two little boys climbing on the broken jungle gym and a middle-aged woman leaning against a tall tree watching them. Was this the hope Trevor was talking about?

"Told you," a warm voice spoke from behind her. She turned to see Trevor standing beside Nate and Sam.

"Sam!" she cried, taking a quick step towards her sister. Sam flinched and stepped back, grasping Nate's hand. Robyn hesitated but then knelt down and wrapped her sister in her arms. Sam stood stiff.

"I knew you'd be all right," Robyn whispered, standing again. Her vision blurred. She blinked, swiping at a rebel tear.

"It'll be okay," Trevor said. The next thing she knew he was drawing her into his arms, pulling her against him.

Robyn closed her eyes and rested her head on his chest, swallowing hard, trying to draw strength from his arms. It wasn't working. She was drowning.

"What? I saved your life and your sister's, and *he* gets the hug," Nate said.

She glanced past Trevor to him. He grinned wryly.

"Thank you for my sister," she said.

"See the kids playing?" Trevor asked, motioning to the kids behind them.

She knew she should just nod but, instead, she pulled herself away to look up into his face. "Don't you realize it's going to be so much worse for them?" She tried to keep her voice gentle. "When the Members come in and sweep this all away—to have had this once and then lose it—it's so much worse than never to have had freedom at all."

"You don't know that," he said. "You've always been free."

"We need to get going," Nate said, interrupting them. "Trevor, you should warn all these folks. The Grims will be looking for us, and they're going to look *everywhere*, especially in places they think are abandoned."

Trevor's face fell as Nate's words seemed to sink in.

Robyn knew what he was thinking. Suddenly, all the safe places that had been rising up in the city were compromised. They'd be looking for them because of Jared. They'd be going through all those neighborhoods they'd given up on, searching homes, finding the pockets of resistance and hope. It was their fault. Her fault.

"Okay. I'll go through here and then hit a few other places, too—let them know what's coming. Nate, you take Robyn and Sam to John's," Trevor said.

"Is that the friend you mentioned?" Robyn asked.

"Yeah," Nate said. "Trev gave me the directions while we were waiting for you. Man, what that information would be worth to the Grims!"

Trevor shot him a look but didn't say anything. He got on his bike.

"Just get them there fast," Trevor said, before riding over to the woman watching the children. He spoke to her before continuing his route.

The woman called to her children and ran toward the houses with them.

"Let's go," Nate said, then started in the other direction.

Robyn walked her bike alongside of him. Sam wouldn't look at her.

"Who is John?" Robyn asked as they turned down an unfamiliar street.

"'John Ashwood. Biggest reason the Independents are still thriving. He has some kind of system of intel going. Keeps tabs on gang movement, temporary safe zones, that kind of thing. There's also a rumor that he has a way of getting people out on the northeast side."

"The northeast?"

"Yeah. Somehow gets them across the river, past No Man's Land, and through the provincial park, to the garrison. That's what they say, anyway."

The garrison?

After the blackout, things got so bad, so quickly. She'd heard that most areas outside the city were now worse than inside, with raiders and wild animals. In the city, the gangs kept things in order. It was bad, but outside was death. Except for maybe the garrison.

"Is that place for real?" she asked.

"Don't know. But if the rumors are true, it's where we want to be."

Could the garrison actually be real? She tried not to give in to the hope, but she felt it. She'd heard about it from some guy in the exchange a year back, some kid who was trying to trade goods for information. When she hadn't taken his offer, he'd told her about it anyway. Like the information was too good to keep inside.

The garrison, he'd said, was in the northeast, across the wide river that snaked along the west perimeter of the city, past the field on the other side, and through the thickly treed provincial park. The word was farmers had banded together shortly after the blackout, knowing how people became after chaos. The ones with older technology on their farms—those who didn't require the power machines of the modern day—had helped the others dig ditches and build walls. They were hunters, too, and heavily armed.

One of the Grims had grabbed the kid then, dragged him away. She hadn't seen him again. She'd almost forgotten his story. But now … If someone was getting people out safely, helping them to this garrison, it was no wonder the gangs silenced the boy.

She studied Nate's face.

"And Trevor just gave his address to you?" she asked.

"He did."

"Why would he do that?"

"Because there is nowhere safe for you now. He knows it. He knows I can get you there. I know where the Grims ride, how to avoid them."

She stopped walking. "Or maybe you're just confirming his address for yourself before turning us in. Maybe you have no intention of helping us."

He whipped around to face her, his eyes flashing anger. "I saved your life."

"Yeah, maybe, but for all I know, you told them where to find us in the first place."

"Me? Because of you, I don't have a home to go back to!" His voice shook. "Because of you, I don't have a family. Do you realize that? They were my *family!*"

"Some family." The words popped out before she could stop them.

He didn't respond. Instead, he just turned and started walking again, still holding Sam's hand.

"Listen," he said after a moment, his voice steady again, "I'm not pretending to help you out of some great kindness here. To be honest, I couldn't care less about you and your little sister. But I'm marked now. I need to get out of this city probably more than you do. Everyone knows me. They know what I look like, and I can't exactly blend in." He held up his gloved, deformed hand and emphasized his limp in his next step. "Yeah, they'll have some people drawing your pictures, circulating them around, but at least they won't know you from a distance. You could maybe find a place to blend in."

She didn't reply. Maybe wasn't good enough.

As they crossed over a main street, she realized she was in a new territory. She yanked the red bandana from her head as two blue-clad Members rode by. The sight was so common now. Two years earlier, they'd be riding motorbikes or modified low riders. Now, what was once a symbol of innocence, of physical ability and agility, of freedom, was twisted into another thing used to control people.

"What are you doing?" Nate whispered to her. "Put it back. You can't have that thing without it."

She did as he told her. "Aren't they going to wonder what I'm doing here?"

"They won't care. We have a truce. Just keep moving. Don't look around. Just go."

One foot in front of the other. She got too close to the bike and the pedal scraped along her calf. Biting her lip, she ignored the sharp pain shooting up her leg.

Nate picked up speed, limping out in front of her. Sam still clutched his hand, her short legs moving twice as quickly to keep up. Nate obviously wanted to get out of the open as much as Robyn did.

It stung to watch her sister shut her out and choose a Grim. She focused on keeping the bike straight.

Suddenly, Nate pulled Sam back, ducking with her around a corner. Robyn could instantly see why. Three figures walked towards her, and as they neared, she made out two guys and a girl, all around her age. They wore blue bandanas, and they were looking in her direction. She swallowed hard.

Confident. You are confident.

She stopped walking as they reached her. "Hey," she said, trying for a casual tone.

"Hey." The boy closest to her nodded. "Heard you guys had some trouble out on your end."

"Yep." She forced herself to meet his eyes.

"So what are you doing over here?" the girl asked.

"Looking for our fugitives." Did they call them that or did they have some sort of official name she didn't know? Their expressions didn't change.

"Your rider already let us know what to watch for," the boy said. "We've been circling around here." He eyed her bike. "Why aren't you riding?"

"Pulled a muscle," she lied quickly. "I'm trying to walk it out. Anyway, I'll let you get back to it."

"Okay. If they come through here, we'll find them."

"Great." She paused. They were waiting for her to clear out of their territory. "Do you mind if I just rest up here a bit before heading back? I don't want to push it too hard, and I'd rather not have to walk it back. If I sit it out for a bit, I should be able to ride back in a few."

"Sure." They started walking again, getting closer to where Sam and Nate had pulled off.

"Hey," she called. "I was supposed to check out the north

side of your territory. I don't suppose you guys could follow up on that for me?"

"Sure." The girl jumped at the tip. "Let's go," she said to the others. They continued walking past the lane hiding Nate and Sam. When they got to the next street, they turned left.

Robyn held her breath until they were gone. Steadying herself on her bike, she waited until Nate and Sam emerged from the alleyway.

"Nice one," Nate said, his voice calm.

Sam was a little pale, and Robyn could tell she'd been frightened.

Without another word, they continued moving, with Sam and Nate hugging the curb a little more closely.

CHAPTER 11

They'd slowed their paced and it was his fault. Nate wished he wasn't limping so heavily. Every few moments, Robyn glanced at him, a worried frown creasing her forehead. His leg hurt, and his unbalanced gate was affecting his back.

He broke the silence, pointing up ahead of them. "We're getting pretty close now."

They were in a residential area, but not like the one Trevor loved so much, the one with the small, squat, decrepit houses. This one had obviously once been suburbia. They turned down a main road, the crumbling brick sign and empty gate hinges signifying the entranceway to the once-gated community. Soon, it broke off into a labyrinth of cul-de-sacs and bays. The fires that had burned in the city center had reached this area as well. Entire neighborhoods were gone. But some streets remained untouched. Here, in the daylight, it was as if there'd never been a blackout at all. Only the overgrown yards and shattered windows betrayed the reality of their situation.

"He lives *here*?" Robyn asked.

"Apparently."

"I thought you said they've been looking for this guy."

"Crews of Members will have swept these houses. And they'll definitely have collected dues from everybody here, especially in an area like this, but they wouldn't have been able to identify Ashwood even if they'd seen him. Nobody really knows what he looks like, outside of a couple of sketches. And even those aren't that helpful."

"And what's your plan?" she asked. "We just go to the door and ask for John Ashwood?"

"Something like that."

"And what? They're just going to introduce us to him?"

He shrugged. "Would be nice, wouldn't it?" He turned down a narrow back lane with double garages lining each side. There were no numbers on any of the houses. Paint peeled on most and some were spray-painted with tags. "Said it was the fourth house in. That'd be this one."

He suspected the square lot had once had a fence; most of these houses would have had one. Of course, the wood had long since been torn down and carried away.

They walked through the tall brown grass to the door, which stood a few feet off the ground. The deck was gone as well.

Nate knocked twice, a slight pause in between each rap. A woman, maybe in her mid-twenties, opened the door. Her thick black hair was pulled back in a low ponytail.

"Can I help you with something?" She raised her eyebrows at them. Her glance lingered on Robyn and her bike.

"Yeah. Trevor West sent us," Nate said. "We're looking for John Ashwood."

"John who?" Her dark eyes narrowed. The woman was doing a poor job of hiding the hostility she felt towards them, and it took Nate a moment to realize the reason: Robyn still wore the red bandana.

"It's not hers." Nate tilted his head towards the rag. "But you know Trevor, don't you? At least let us wait here for him."

"Trevor?" the woman asked, no attempt to hide the hostility this time. When Nate didn't answer, she added, "Never mind. I'm sorry. Go wait somewhere else. I can't help you."

Nate wasn't planning on going anywhere, and the woman's hand, which had been resting on her hip, had moved behind her back. No doubt she was armed.

"Please," Sam said, startling them. "We walked all the way across the city. Bad people are looking for us." Her voice cracked, and suddenly there were tears streaming down her face. "They killed my friend."

The resolve on the woman's face wavered. He could tell she was thinking either they were genuinely in need, or this was an award-winning performance.

He tried honesty. "I'm Nate Cooper. Trevor's my best— only friend. We just—"

"Oh. Cooper. I know who you are." She moved out of the entranceway. From her expression, whatever she knew about him wasn't good. "The three of you, come inside. Now." They walked in past her. She added, "John's not here, but I'll see if I can send word to him."

If Nate knew one thing, he knew lies. It was clear to him this woman wasn't telling the truth. Either she was planning to send word to the gangs and turn them in, or Ashwood was in one of the other rooms right now, no more than a few feet away from them.

"Sure. You do that."

They started at the sound of two knocks on the door, the same pattern as Nate's. The door opened and Trevor came in, pulling in his bike. "You made it. You okay?" His gaze scanned Nate's damaged leg.

"I'm fine."

"It was a *really* long walk," Sam said, looking at Trevor.

"Danika." Trevor turned to the dark-haired woman. "Have you taken them to meet John yet?"

"No," she said. "I don't know them."

"Right. This is Robyn." Trevor touched Robyn lightly on the arm. He left his hand there as he continued. "And this is her sister, Sam, and you know about Nate already."

Nate tried not to think about Trevor's hand on Robyn.

"I do. Hi." Danika's voice was flat. "I thought you said Nate still worked for—"

"I know. But they got in some serious trouble earlier today with the Members. The gangs are looking for them, pretty much city-wide now. I was getting word out to some of the Friendlies. Let them know there'd be sweeps."

"What did these three do to have the gangs doing *city-wide* sweeps?"

"Grims came for Robyn's bike last night," Nate said. "Pretty sure they weren't planning to just take it and go."

"And?" Danika raised her eyebrows.

"Jared Ward is dead."

The words hung in the air as Danika seemed to let the implications sink in. "That kid was probably all Marshall had." Her voice held no pity, but it trembled slightly. "Do you have any idea what he'll do when he finds the people responsible?" She looked at Trevor. "And anyone who helps them?"

"I know," Robyn said.

"It didn't help when they realized I was involved," Nate said. He pointed to the bandana on Robyn's head. "That's mine, in case you didn't know."

"You're not making things any better," Robyn whispered as Danika grabbed Trevor's arm and pulled him aside, muttering something.

"Not trying to." Nate shrugged. He pulled the bandana off Robyn's head and shoved the corner into his pocket, letting the rest hang out. "They might as well know what they're getting into if they're going to try to help us."

Danika sighed. "Trevor trusts you. We're betting our lives on it here, so …" She seemed to be making a decision. "Follow me. I'll take you to John. You can leave that bike here. Trevor will stash it in the room with his. He'll make sure it's safe." She abruptly turned and, after Robyn handed off the bike, they followed her down the hallway, through the kitchen, and to the basement stairs.

It was pitch black as they descended. Nate ran his hand along the wall to steady himself. There was no banister.

"Window wells were filled in a long time ago," Danika said, "so nobody could sneak into the basement through them. Makes for a good hiding place. Here, does someone have a light?"

Nate fumbled in his pocket. His fingers found the Zippo lighter and he flicked it on. With the little flame, he could make out a smallish basement devoid of furniture. It had cement walls and floor, with an unfinished ceiling.

They walked down the rest of the stairs into the room. The windows were, as Danika had said, completely black. Danika led them over to where a small gas fireplace stood against a brick wall. Grasping the edges of it, she pulled it away from the wall, the stone bottom scraping against the floor. It was an after-market fireplace placed in an artificial wall.

"Nice," he said.

"We have creative people here. You can do anything if you need to," Danika said. "We took the bricks from demolished houses down the street, stacked them up, made a sort of mortar to stick them together. Drywall would have been easier, but most of the hardware stores burned down in the fires. The ones that didn't were raided pretty heavily by the time we thought of this. The fireplace is from the house next door. Nobody was there to use it when we found it."

"How do you breathe down here?" Robyn asked.

"We opened up and expanded the dryer vents," Danika said. "The room in here used to be the laundry room. Quiet now." She ducked low and led them into the hidden room.

The room was lit by three small candles. Several bikes—mountain, BMX, road— hung on the room's walls.

It was tempting. If he had something like one of these to trade, he might find a Member who would give him a pass for it, help him out despite Marshall's directive. Greed was currency. He forced the thought away. Trevor was risking everything for him.

About a dozen people were inside the room. They sat on the floor, listening intently to the speaker who was crouched down in the midst of them. His voice carried through the still room.

"People," he was saying as they came in, "the Enemy wants you to be afraid. He wants you to roll over and give up. He wants you to feel abandoned and hopeless, but we don't need to be afraid."

Nate grinned as he realized what John Ashwood was doing. The man was *preaching*. He wanted to laugh out loud at the irony—a message about having no fear, delivered while hidden in a dark basement room with no window.

"The gangs want you to think they own those streets,

that they own this city," the man said, bringing his voice down slightly, although it still wasn't at an appropriate level for the size of the space they were crammed into. "But they don't. Yeah, protect yourself. Yeah, be safe. Be cautious. But don't waste your time being afraid. Remember, 'God has not given us a spirit of fear but of power and of love and of a sound mind' and 'He who is within you is greater than he who is in the world.'" He looked up at Danika. She must have signaled to him because he said, "And I guess, with that, we'll wrap up for now."

Nate had gone to Mass before, with an aunt. He expected the man to end with some sort of long, drawn out prayer. Instead, all he did was quickly extend his hand over the crowd, his eyes open, and say, "May the Lord bless you and keep you safe during these dark times." The small crowd murmured an Amen and then, as Danika moved out of the way, filed out one by one.

"Where will they go?" Robyn whispered to Trevor, who had come down with them.

"To their homes. They'll be careful."

"They don't live here?"

"This isn't a commune," he said. "Actually, it belongs to Danika and her husband. John sleeps in a spare room upstairs, and sometimes other people stay here if they need to. They also have some medical equipment stashed in the walls. Not much, but we managed to salvage a few of the leftovers from Hope Memorial, the stuff the gangs missed, before the fires. Syringes, needles, gauze, thread. Some antibiotics and specialty kits. When people come to us, we don't turn anyone away. We even have a nurse—Stacie—who volunteers to help a few times a week."

Nate saw Robyn glance up at Trevor, a question in her eyes at the way Trevor had said the name.

Robyn raised her eyebrows. "Stacie, hey?"

"You brought guests," John said, looking up. He stood, and Nate was struck by how tall and broad the man was. On the floor, he'd blended in with the rest of the people but, now, he stood at least a head above even Trevor, who had to be around six feet himself. His beard was full, bushy, and almost black, matching his thick dark eyebrows, which seemed to make his light blue eyes even stranger. His hair, a nondescript brown, was long and almost straight, hanging down past his shoulders. He smiled at them as he approached—a wide, full-toothed smile—and the lines around his eyes told them it was genuine.

"Hey there," he said as he extended his hand to Nate. Nate shook it, not meeting John's eyes. The man exuded power. Nate hadn't felt intimidated in a long time. He didn't like it.

John moved to shake Robyn's hand next, and then, crouching down, eye-level with Sam, he shook hers as well. "And what's your name?" he asked her, warmth in his voice.

"Sam," she said, "and this is my friend, Nate." She paused and John waited for her to finish. She sighed. "And this is my sister, Robyn."

"Well, it's very nice to meet you." He stood and shifted his gaze back to Nate and Robyn. "All of you. Now, what can I do for you?"

Nate cleared his throat. "Reverend—" he started, but John's deep, throaty chuckle interrupted him and he stopped abruptly.

"I'm sorry," John said, grinning and shaking his head. "I don't think I've ever been called a reverend before."

Nate shoved his hands in his pockets, shrugging. "Rabbi?" He eyed John's beard.

"I'm no teacher either," John said, patting Nate on the shoulder. "Just love sharing the Word."

Okay, Ashwood was somewhat fanatical. Maybe a little

crazy. "We came here because we need help." Nate gave up guessing a title.

"We could all use some of that," John said. "Although I suspect you mean help with something specific."

"We're hoping." Nate was uncomfortable as he answered. Robyn had her hands shoved in her pockets. She looked as awkward as he felt. John Ashwood wasn't what he'd been expecting at all. "We need to get out."

John nodded. "What time frame are we looking at?"

"I don't know," Trevor said, "but they'll be actively combing the city for them. We'll want to get word out to the Independents, too. There'll be more heat for a while."

"Vargas is out on a run right now with some of the others. He should be back sometime after nightfall, before morning."

"Who's Vargas?" Sam asked.

"Vargas" —John smiled down on her— "is Max Vargas, Danika's husband. He's one of the men we're blessed to have working with us and the only one who knows how to get people out of the northeast side of the city. Trust me, little lady, with Vargas on the case, you and your family here will have no problem getting out."

"We're not—" Robyn started.

Sam interrupted her. "Thanks."

John nodded again. "So," he said, looking at Nate and Robyn, "I guess you're going to need some place to stay until Max can finalize the exit plans. There's a spare room upstairs for emergencies. If you three don't mind sharing the space, that is."

"Thanks," Robyn said.

"No problem," John said. "If it's okay with you, though, after you're settled, I'd like to talk to you two alone."

Trevor hung back with John as Danika led them back

upstairs and then to a large, second floor room lit by an oversized window. Even with no pillow and no other furniture, the clean, well-kept place seemed like a luxury suite.

Nate glanced at Robyn. She looked at her sister, who was eyeing the bed. Sam stifled a yawn. No wonder the little girl was exhausted. She'd had next to no sleep and had spent a good part of the day walking.

"Sweetie, can I tuck you in?" Robyn asked.

There was a long silence. "Okay." Sam looked at the floor. It was the first thing she'd said to Robyn since they'd left Nate's place.

The silent treatment must have been killing Robyn, Nate guessed. He knew why Sam was angry. She felt Robyn had abandoned her. But Sam would figure it out soon enough—Robyn would always do whatever it took to protect her sister.

Robyn walked over to the bed and pulled back the covers. Sam crawled in and let Robyn tuck the covers in all around her. Nate turned to stare out the window. These loose ends had grown on him. He couldn't explain it, even to himself.

"Will you come back?" Sam's voice was heavy with sleep.

"Promise," Robyn said.

"Really promise?"

"Really, really promise." Fabric rustled as Robyn leaned over to kiss Sam good night.

"Stay with me till I fall asleep," she said, her words already slurring together.

"'Okay." The bed groaned as Robyn sat down on the edge.

Nate left the room. Where to now? He didn't know this place. Did he really want to wander around alone?

"You coming or what?" he finally called from the doorway. He heard her sigh and stand.

"I guess. Sam's passed out already." Robyn joined him in the hallway. "Why do I feel so nervous?"

"Because the guy we're trusting to get us out of here is a complete nut job?"

"Come on."

"Seriously. Leading, what, some kind of a cult in the basement?"

"You're the one who called him a reverend."

He shrugged. "Sounded like one to me."

"Like one what?" As they reached the foot of the stairs, John was waiting for them, leaning against the wall.

"A reverend," Nate muttered.

John grinned again. "Thanks, I guess."

"Why do you do that?" Robyn asked. "You know, the meetings in the basement?"

"We used to meet in the street," John said, "but people kept getting killed. I don't know why. It wasn't the religion really that specifically bothered them. At least, as far as I could tell."

"We don't like people having hope, whatever form it's in," Nate said. Might as well clear things up. "It wasn't the meetings; it was the *result* of the meetings. Hope, faith—bad for business."

"Makes sense." John nodded, almost to himself. "Anyway, eventually everyone stopped coming. We figured God would understand if we took things underground for a while. The early church did the same thing."

"What, met in the basement behind a fireplace?" Nate chuckled.

"Probably not. But met in secret, sure."

"Hey, man, no judgment here," Nate said, putting up his hands in mock surrender. "You do what you gotta do."

"I know." John shrugged. "But it won't always be this way.

Either enough people will stand up and fight for our city, or it will just … explode. The gangs and their Members may be running things, but they're not running things for sustainability. The way things are, they can't last forever."

Nate nodded. The man wasn't wrong. He glanced at Robyn, catching her eye. She seemed to be waiting for his reaction to John's statement. Maybe she expected him to disagree, to defend the Members? After all, until last night, he'd been one of them. Then again, he'd been helping her become an Independent and keeping Trevor's route hidden from his own crew. And he'd killed Members to protect her and her sister. She had to know he didn't have loyalties anymore.

"What are you looking at?" Nate asked her, and he thought he saw her cheeks redden before she looked away.

"Nothing."

CHAPTER 12

"Come on, kids. Sitting room's this way." It was funny to hear John refer to them as kids and to easily accept the designation. If Robyn hadn't already met him and liked him, she'd have resented it. After all, he couldn't be much older than thirty and, with the way the world was now, she and Nate were hardly children. It was also strange to hear him refer to a sitting room, a name her grandma had given to a room in her house back in California. Sure enough, though, he led them into a small room with two wide armchairs and what had to be at least a fifteen-inch television.

"The TV just makes it feel homey. Nobody wanted to get rid it of," John said. He sat down in one of the chairs.

Nate sat down in the other one, but slid over, trying to make room for her. She ignored the small space left beside him and elected to sit on the large armrest, placing her feet down beside him instead.

"So, fill me in," John said.

Nate cleared his throat. "Guess it started when the Grims—some of my crew—shot an Independent a while back. I heard the gunshot and looked out my window."

He saw me. He saw what I did. Robyn pictured the dying cyclist looking up at her, begging her with his eyes to help him.

"He was already dead, so she grabbed the bike and took off," Nate said, and Robyn released her held breath in a quiet rush. So Nate didn't know she'd left the man to die. It's not like she could have saved the rider's life anyway and it was a chance—a real chance—to help her own family. Who wouldn't have done exactly what she'd done? Still, the idea that nobody else knew was a relief.

"I saw her face, and I already knew where she lived." Nate held up his useless hand. "I'm not good for much else besides intel. Have a pretty good memory. A really good memory. I'd seen her around plenty at the market, followed her home a few times."

It chilled her to hear him casually admit to stalking her. He'd known where she lived the whole time and hadn't threatened her or contacted her at all until she had something specific he wanted.

John leaned forward, his elbows resting on his knees, his thumbs firmly pressed together while he tapped the tips of his forefingers. "So you're an intel man. And now you're here." John was obviously aware of the danger that Nate posed and the price on his own head.

"Yeah, it'd be a pretty big score for me, right?" Nate shook his head. "Worthless now though. Wish I'd thought of it earlier, before things went sideways. What I did, the Grims—and Marshall—can't forgive."

"Okay." John leaned back. "Tell me, what did you do?"

Nate summarized the last two days' events, painting a thorough picture about how they'd gotten here.

It was so strange, listening to him talk about how he'd killed those men like it was nothing, like they meant nothing to him, despite the fact he'd told her earlier they were like his family.

John's expression didn't change. His thick eyebrows were furrowed and he nodded every few minutes. Nate finished with their arrival; John was silent.

Robyn couldn't think of anything to add. It was up to John to figure out what to do now. Did he consider them murderers? It was self-defense. He had to get that. She pictured again the Independent in the alleyway. She hadn't killed him, but she was pretty sure this man of God sitting across from her, with his deep convictions and religious certainty, would find her actions that night repulsive.

She shook the thought off. No guilt for her, thanks.

"You were right about the urgency of your situation," John said finally. "Jared was a very important boy to his father. In spite of everything, I'm sorry for his loss. Whatever faults your gang leader has—and he has lots of them—not loving his own kid has never been one of them. It's gotta hit a man hard." He stood and sighed. "It's a tragedy, for sure."

Robyn didn't detect any blame in his voice, only an underpinning of sorrow and sympathy for the dead man's family.

Nate must've caught it, too, because he thrust out his chin. "I told you they killed that old woman. And they would have killed me and taken Robyn and the little girl. You know what my crew does to girls they take as prisoners, don't you?" He didn't have to elaborate. "What, you believe this God of yours thinks we should have let them take us? You think He disapproves of us defending ourselves against people like that?"

"I never said anything like that," John said, his voice remaining calm. "But just because something seems necessary or justified doesn't make it any less tragic."

He reached out to put his hand on Nate's arm but Nate jerked back and laughed. Robyn knew the tone. "It doesn't matter. It's not like those two are the only people I've killed. I was in the gang before the blackout. What do you think initiation was? You think I just paid a fee and signed up? Man, I signed in blood. You know that, Preacher?" He used the term like an insult. "And after the blackout, I was a full-out Member. I'd still be one if it weren't for the fire. You're down here in your little hiding place, telling people not to be afraid, and, really, the people they're afraid of are exactly like me."

John waited for him to finish. Robyn had no idea what had gotten into Nate. It had to be something about John's sympathy that set him off.

"You sit there and listen and feel bad for Jared and Rob and me, but there was nothing good in them," Nate said. "And there's sure as hell nothing good in me."

John looked at him. "Nobody's good but God alone," he said. "I accepted that about myself a long time ago."

Nate opened his mouth to reply but seemed to change his mind, turning his back. He stumbled as he limped towards the door, leaving without a word.

"I'm so sorry," Robyn said after he'd gone. "I don't know what—"

"Guy's carrying around a load of guilt."

"Nate? Nate doesn't feel bad about anything. He's proud of it." Even as she said it, she wasn't sure. *Is he really?*

"He's not proud of it. Maybe he wants people to think he is, but I know shame when I see it, and that's shame."

"Are you still going to help us?"

"Of course."

She hesitated before asking her next question. "And Nate, too, right?" She didn't know why it mattered. Nate didn't do any of this for them, and he'd just finished laying out all the reasons for her to want to get as much distance from him as possible.

"Nate too," John said.

"Thanks."

"Maybe you should get some sleep. I'll talk to Max as soon as he gets in and we'll start working on a concrete plan to get you guys out."

In her room, she found Nate standing at the window, his hand on the window frame, looking out onto the street. At the sound of her footsteps, he turned around to face her. The hard expression on his face was gone, and he seemed almost vulnerable in the fading light.

"Is he kicking me out?" he asked, running the toe of his shoe along the floor. She shook her head. "Don't know why I freaked." He leaned back against the wall. "He started talking about how it was such a tragedy and everything and I just lost it. Guess it was just like, man, it's no tragedy. Nobody should care that they're gone." He turned to look out the window again. His voice was softer and she almost had to strain to hear it. "When they finally catch me—and they will, I know it—when they put a bullet in my head, do you think I expect people to call it a tragedy? Nobody's gonna cry for me. People like Jared and Rob and me, we're the same."

Robyn crossed the room and stood beside him at the window. The street was quiet and still, although there were faint lights burning within some of the once-opulent houses. "John says it's not that simple."

"John's not all there, if you know what I mean. *You* know what I am."

She did. Of course she did. A day ago, she hated him. She looked out at the setting sun. It was getting colder, and she wrapped her arms around herself. Although this house had most of its windows intact and she'd noticed an ornate wood-burning fireplace off the main hallway, it was freezing.

"You should go lie down with Sam before you get too cold," he said, glancing over at her.

"What are you going to do?" she asked.

"Sleep is overrated."

Robyn looked back towards where Sam slept, tucked in the large bed against the wall. Nate would be standing there all alone, as the night got colder. His leg must be killing him after walking all day.

"You can sleep on the other side of me if you want," she said, surprising herself with the offer. He didn't need her permission. She hadn't even realized she was going to say it, but something about John's reaction to Nate made her think. Somehow, she knew he wasn't any threat to her, and it was crazy to let anyone freeze when there was a bed big enough for the three of them.

"Yeah?" He raised his eyebrows as he turned to face her.

"Guess so. But just sleeping."

He didn't laugh like she thought he would but nodded, avoiding her eyes. "That's decent of you. I may take you up on that if I sleep tonight." He faced the window. "Night, Robyn."

It was the first time she'd actually heard him use her name.

Robyn climbed underneath the blanket and moved herself over so she was right up against Sam. Looking up at the ceiling, she willed herself to fall asleep. It didn't happen, even as the room darkened and the sun set. Finally, Nate crossed the room. The bed sagged as he climbed in beside her, clearly careful not to touch her. He turned on his side, facing away from her and resting his head on his forearm, leaving a sliver of space between them. She was grateful for his tact. Even with the gap, warmth emanated from him, and she was grateful for that, too. The temperature was dropping and she could use all the warmth she could get. After a while, she felt Nate relax beside her. His breathing deepened as he fell asleep. The room continued to darken around them until nothing was visible but the pale gray of moonlight filtering through the window.

An image of her mother came back to her, of crawling into her bed after a bad dream. Her mother had always smelled like lilacs. She forced the image from her mind. Her mother was gone, and it was because of men like the one laying next to her. She tried to feel the hatred she'd felt when she'd first met him, the hatred she should have felt when he reacted so violently to John's compassion. She tried to feel again how she'd felt the last time she'd seen him sleeping, when she'd thought about using the knife she had in her pocket. But she didn't feel like that anymore. Had she grown soft? What had changed?

She turned her head to rest her cheek on the cool of the bed, trying to ignore the tousled mess of hair beside her. What was it she actually felt towards him now? Not indifference. For whatever reason, he saved her life and her sister's. She didn't understand him, but she trusted him. What would he have been like if he had made the same choices Trevor had? She hadn't understood the friendship before. She'd been hung up on wondering how someone like Trevor, who was honest and kind, could ever stay friends with a person like Nate, and how he could have just revealed John's location on nothing but Nate's word. But now she could see it. It still didn't make any sense to her, but, somehow, she understood. Nate wasn't a good man, and he didn't pretend to be. But there was a remnant there, of something, or someone, who might be. Never in a million years would she have imagined herself willingly sharing a bed with a Member. But somehow, in the cold of the room and with the uncertainty of the future, she was.

***

Robyn opened her eyes at a quick, frantic banging on the front door downstairs. The early morning light filtered in from the window. The banging stopped for a brief moment, and then continued in a slower, controlled rhythm. One-two. Pause. One-Two. Pause. She sat up, the cold air hitting her as the blanket fell from her shoulders. Footsteps sounded past her door and down the stairs. The front door opened. Muffled, hurried voices carried up from the entranceway.

Nate stirred beside her. "What's going on?" His voice was still hoarse with sleep. He sat up and swung his legs over the side of the bed and listened with her to the action downstairs.

"Are you going to check it out?" she whispered.

"Yeah, just give me a second." He massaged his bad leg. After a moment, he rose, unsteady. "Stay here."

She was already standing. "You know that's not going to happen." She tucked the blanket tight around her still-sleeping sister and hurried to catch up with him. She followed him down the stairs and into the kitchen.

Danika was collapsed on a chair, her head on the table. John had his hand on her back and was leaning towards her while he spoke to two men Robyn had never seen before and to Trevor, who stood just behind them. His face had lost its color.

Danika looked up, hearing Robyn and Nate come in. She stood, knocking the chair back. It hit the floor with a crash and she stepped towards Nate, eyes wet.

"This is *your* fault," she spat, pointing her finger at his chest.

One of the men, older and almost as tall as John but somehow not as imposing, put a hand on her shoulder. "Won't help things."

Danika shook him off. "You don't understand, Elijah. He's *one of them.*"

He dropped his hand, shaking his head and then running his fingers through tight black curls. "He's …" His eyes shifted to Nate's face, which had become expressionless. A mask.

"What happened?" Robyn asked.

"They took him!" Danika said, fresh tears spilling down her cheeks.

"They took Max," the smaller of the two men behind Trevor said. Robyn looked at the kid speaking. He had a striking resemblance to the other man, but he was a lot younger. Eleven, maybe twelve, at the most. "He was with his team, so they got Aaron, Bryant, and Stacie, too. Grims were doing a sweep of the area, and they found the bikes stashed in their apartment. Dad and I got out of there, but they took the others. It looked bad."

"We'll get them back, Calvin." John said.

"Get them back?" Nate asked. Robyn felt her face flush in embarrassment. "You can't be serious. After the Members have them …"

"We are serious," John said firmly. "In the meantime, Danika, please go and let the families know we need to evacuate, and then pack up as quickly as you can."

She walked past them, bumping Nate hard with her shoulder.

"Elijah and Calvin," John said to the father and son team who had been with Max, "go get all the bikes. We'll need to make sure we still have them when it's time to go for Max and the others. And grab the med kit."

"Why are we leaving?" Robyn asked.

"Our people know what's at stake if they give up information. But they also know I don't expect them to die protecting us."

"The gangs already know that most Independents get help from John so they'd assume the Independents can tell them where he is," Nate said. "They probably also know we're trying to get out so John's not the only big ticket here. They'll torture them until they find out where we are, and then they'll kill them."

"Max will hold out until he dies," John said. "His wife is here, but the others … We're friends, but they're human. It won't be long until the Grims come for us."

The two men disappeared down another hallway just off the kitchen.

Trevor didn't hesitate. "Time to go, Robyn. Go get Sam. Coop, help me pack up some supplies."

Nate nodded, moving towards Trevor as Robyn spun around and hurried back up the stairs. It was their fault this was happening. They both knew it. She wasn't sure if Nate cared, but she did. If she hadn't stolen the bike in the first place, or if she'd just been more careful not to lead them to her …

She took the stairs two at a time.

CHAPTER 13

They weren't traveling as far as Robyn expected but, once outside, they went much slower than she would have liked. The men moved the bikes one at a time. She wasn't sure she would get hers back. The rest of them went on foot, separately. John and Sam walked together. He looked like he could be her father, holding her hand as they disappeared down the street first. She, Danika, and Trevor followed later, taking a different route to the same place. They gave Nate directions to the house, too, but they left him to find his own way. Robyn hadn't liked it, but he'd insisted. His limp and deformed hand made him easy to recognize, and he said it would be easier for him to stay out of sight on his own.

Now, she stood by the large front window, peering out. Sam stood beside her, holding her hand. Nate could just take off. Or maybe he'd just turn himself—or them—in. Maybe he'd try to buy himself some grace.

The place they'd settled in was devoid of most furniture. She'd taken a tour already. Nothing left in the living room. A small, rectangular table stood in the center of the attached kitchen, with a few pots and a steel spatula sitting under a rusted and stained sink. The hallway off the kitchen led to what must have been the bedrooms. One still had floral curtains hanging over its square window and all three still had beds. She wondered where the original occupants were. The house hadn't been raided or gutted. But the people who'd once lived here had disappeared. Everybody did eventually, one way or another. She shuddered. That was why she and Sam were going to get out. No matter what. And she knew she needed Nate to do it.

***

It had to be about midday, from the color of the skyline. She looked away from the window to the group gathered in the kitchen. John huddled around the small wooden table with Danika and Trevor, and Elijah and Calvin, who had returned from stashing the bikes. Robyn couldn't really hear what they were saying, but they had paper and a pencil out and she could tell they were trying to sketch a map. As she'd suspected, it was pointless without Nate. It was Nate's crew that had them, and he would know their base better than anyone. She already knew she was going to go with them. She needed Max to get her and Sam out of the city, and there was no way she'd risk having the rescue fail.

Her sister pulled Robyn's arm. "Nate's coming here, right?" Sam asked, her eyes fixed down the empty street.

Robyn couldn't make herself respond. Who knew?

She thought instead of the books she left behind. Maybe they'd be able to get more from someone, if they ever got outside. Or maybe they'd write their own someday. Turning away, she gently took her hand out of Sam's and joined the others at the table.

"So what have you figured out?" she asked.

Danika glanced up, pursing her lips. John pointed at

one of the streets he'd drawn around his rendition of the large, sprawling police station the gang leaders used as their primary base of operation. "We'll take the BMXs. Use foot pegs to carry our friends back." Bikes aside, she didn't see how it would work. She didn't know much about the station, but she knew the area behind it was a maze of streets and back alleyways, and that the building was heavily fortified. There would be guards and scouts and snipers. They would never leave anything to chance. The front of it was more or less out in the open because of fire damage to the surrounding buildings. No sneaking up on it that way. Getting people out wasn't possible.

"He's here!" Sam called from the window, then ran to the door.

"Wait!" Robyn said.

Sam ignored her, swinging open the door and running out into the street. Robyn ran after her but stopped in the doorway and leaned against the frame. Sam had thrown herself at Nate, hugging him around his waist and burying her face in his shirt. Nate awkwardly patted her back. Then, with the same hand, he reached into his cargo pants and pulled out a thin, ragged-looking comic book. The cover was torn and the edges of the pages were frayed and yellowed, but it was intact. Sam gasped.

"Found it on the way. Knew a little girl who loves books." Nate handed it to her.

She grabbed it with both hands.

He looked past her at Robyn and the small crowd that had followed her to the door. "You guys the welcoming party or what?" He limped past them into the house.

Sam took the book and went to curl up beside the window.

The rest continued on to the kitchen.

"So you think you're really gonna save this guy?" Nate asked.

"I do," John replied. "We're going to bring all four of them back."

"You know it's impossible."

"With God, anything is possible."

"Don't you mean, with me, anything is possible? I mean, you are planning to ask me how to get in there, right?" Nate gestured to the map.

"Who do you think sent you here?" John asked with a smile.

Robyn was pretty sure he wasn't kidding.

"Now," John said, "come show us how to do this."

Nate obliged, coming over to take a closer look at the crude drawing. "You got it kind of wrong here," he said, grabbing the pencil and correcting the street names and some of the angles. Then, he started placing Xs. "These are the lookouts. There'll be lots of them."

"Will they be armed?" Robyn asked.

"What do you think?" Now he drew a darker line. "There's a narrow path you can take. Here, it's not so heavily guarded because it's hard to find. The entrance to the path will have one guard at the most. Sometimes nobody watches it. It's between these two buildings. You'll barely be able to see it, especially if it's dark. When you get halfway through, you'll need to turn again. There are a few paths that come off this alley, but it's the third."

"Are you coming with us?" Elijah asked.

"No can do." Nate held up his hand. "Can't walk, can't ride."

"What makes you think that?" John asked, sounding surprised at Nate's statement.

"It's true. Can't pedal with this foot, it just gets in the way.

And the hand's no good for gripping the handlebar."

"You could use my fixie," John said. "It's a single-gear bike, so you wouldn't have to worry about shifting. And you could ride clipped in. I've got cycling shoes. The cleats just snap into the pedals. Your feet would be locked in. Your bad leg would just follow along with the good. And the key here won't be speed, anyway. Slow's okay."

Robyn knew John was right. Nate could ride.

"He'd fall over if he had to stop suddenly," Trevor said. "He'd never get his cleats unclipped in time."

"Yeah, there's a bit of a trick to getting your feet out, but I'm pretty sure Nate could get the hang of it soon enough. And I'd be willing to bet he can balance fine with one hand."

Nate turned back to the map.

"You could lead us …" Robyn started.

"No way," Nate said. "I'm not going."

"You can do this," John said.

"I said I'm not going." Nate said it forcefully this time. He turned, his gait quick and unsteady as he headed away from them down the nearest hall.

He was afraid. Robyn saw it in his face as he argued against John's offer. But Nate knew the way there and he knew the station inside out. They couldn't go without him. She just had to make him see it.

***

"Nate!" Robyn called as she followed him down the hallway.

He wanted to ignore her. He knew what she was going to try to do.

"Nate!"

He swung around to face her. "What?"

"Where are you going?"

"Away from those idiots trying to convince me to join their suicide mission. That's what it is, you know. Nobody gets in there without the Grims knowing about it."

"But you know how. The rest of these guys barely know Grim territory. None of them live there. You do. And I do. That's why I'm coming too."

She was? "Don't. It's not worth it. We'll find another way out of here. Maybe you don't even need to get out."

"What, and just keep hiding here with Sam? And hope nobody recognizes us—ever? There is no other way. You said so yourself. You said we need John, and John needs Max, so we go get Max."

"You're insane," he said. "If they catch us—"

"If they catch us, at least we'll die doing something good."

"Good?" He laughed. He had to make her see. "What, you're taking the moral high ground now?" He leaned in close to her. "I saw how you got that bike, you know. You think that the Independent you left bleeding out on the road would think you're good?" Her face paled. He'd hit his mark. "Do you know what happened to him after you took off with his bike and the Members found him? Think they gave him a peaceful death?"

She closed her eyes against his words. He could tell she hadn't realized he'd seen her. He hadn't planned to say anything, but it was too late now.

He forged ahead. "What do you think John would say if he knew what you did? Don't talk to me about doing a good thing." He tried one of the doors off the hallway. It swung open to a small bedroom, where light filtered in from the open window. Hobbling in, he sat on the bed and stared up at her. "Are we done now?"

She looked like she wanted to throw up … or run as far

away from him as she could. Instead, she stepped into the room.

"They won't be able to make it without you," she said. "When you showed us that map—Nate, it's going to be so dark and you're the only one who knows the way by heart." She stared at her hands. "I know what I did. I do. I don't think I'm a good person. I just want to get Max home to his wife and then get my sister somewhere safer than this." She met his eyes and it was his turn to look away. She crossed the space between them and sat down on the bed beside him, their shoulders touching. "Please come with me."

"I'm not even sure I can ride a bike anymore, even clipped in."

"I bet you could. You used to ride, right?"

"Yep. Got real good, too."

"What happened? To your hand, I mean?"

He never talked about it, but now it seemed pointless not to. "It was an accident. Not from the city fires. That would have been easier to take, I guess." He held up his hand and carefully pulled off his black glove. The skin around the twisted hand was a mess of red and blistered scar tissue. "I did this to myself, really. We were setting this house on fire, making an example of some guy that wouldn't give us our cut. I was careless. Got myself stuck inside. There was bad nerve damage and I almost died from infection." He offered a half-smile. "I didn't. Just lost most of the function in my hand and leg. And my bike, the respect of the guys, and pretty much every friend I thought I had, except Trev. Poor me, right?" He tried to laugh, but it sounded hollow.

She must have seen he was telling the truth, that he did it to himself. That he deserved what he got. Why had her eyes filled with tears, then?

"You're really not coming?" Trevor asked, appearing in the doorway.

He'd been certain a minute ago there was no way. He'd rather die at the hands of the Grims than get back on a bike and risk the humiliation of being unable to do it. But now … What if they actually needed him?

He sighed. "I guess I can't have you getting caught and ratting me out, right?" Nate slid his glove back onto his hand. "But if you get me killed, you owe me."

"You got it," Trevor said.

"Fine." What did he have to lose anyway? "I'll help. But then Max gets us out of here, right?"

"I promise."

They followed Trevor back to where John and the others were waiting.

"So you're coming, Nate?" John asked.

Nate nodded.

"I am, too," Danika said, but John was interrupting before she finished.

"You're not," John said.

"He's my husband."

"You're not going. I'm sorry. We'll bring him home to you."

"John …"

"Max would never forgive me if I let anything happen to you or that baby," he said with gentle finality.

She put her hand over her stomach. Nate hadn't noticed the curvature of her belly and, from the look on Robyn's face, neither had she.

"How did you know?" Danika asked.

"You rest your hand on it all the time, like you're trying to keep it safe. And sometimes you get this smile … It's like Ellie used to look before she had our little one." He turned to Nate and Robyn. "Ellie's my wife. She and my son were with the first people Max got out. That's how I know he's the best."

"Your family's out there without you?" Robyn asked.

"They are. It wasn't safe for them here."

"Why aren't you out there with them?"

John blinked, clearing the moisture that had gathered in his eyes. "Hoping to join them one of these days, but we felt like God still has work for me here." He tapped the map again. "Starting with this."

"Let me come," Robyn said. "I'm fast. Ask Trevor. I know the territory because I lived near it—nearer than any of you, other than Nate. And you'll want the extra rider. What if you need someone to distract the guards? Or run interference? What if something goes wrong?"

Nate could tell she was winning them over. He wanted to point out *he'd* be there as an extra rider, but he knew he wouldn't be nearly as fast as he needed to be to run any kind of interference, and carrying anyone on the back of his bike would be impossible.

"Or what if something happens to Nate and he can't help with the directions. I'm telling you, I know the area. And I'm good on a bike. Really good. Back home in California, I lived for biking," she added. "I can do this."

"What about your sister?" Trevor asked.

"That's why I have to go." Robyn glanced over at Sam, who was still engrossed in the comic. "Maybe Sam and I could find somewhere else in the city to live, outside the reach of the Grims, but if we could actually get out away from the gangs, that's worth risking. Somewhere Sam could actually be free." She broke off and met Danika's eyes. "Could I leave her with you until I get back?"

"Of course." Danika's hand was on her belly again.

Nate looked at each of the two women in turn. Robyn would see Danika as strong and loyal, with a capacity to love. He knew Robyn trusted Danika to take care of Sam if they didn't make it out. But some things were better left unsaid.

"That's six of us, Nate, including you," John said. "Can we do this with six?"

Nate nodded. "I guess."

"I was thinking we'd use the BMXs. They have foot pegs we could use to bring back the others. More steady and faster than using handlebars, right?" John locked eyes with Robyn. "We have a few different bikes we ride around here—we try to get good at them all, so we can use what we have. You said you rode back home. How are you on a BMX?"

"I used to be awesome," she said. "And it's not something you forget."

"Good. Nate will take the fixie and be guide. Calvin's the quickest, so he'll take the cross bike and run distraction." Robyn glanced up at Elijah. He had to feel something about his own child taking a risk like this, but his expression hadn't changed.

He caught her eye. "John's right. Calvin's a flash on the bike."

She thought about Sam. "But he's ..." she trailed off. *Just a kid? Family?*

"He's my son. A skilled rider." Elijah laid his hand on Calvin's shoulder. "And a young man whose proven himself to be a valuable part of this team. Your little sister there is still pretty young, but I can guarantee it won't be long until she comes into her own. Until you see her as able to make her own calls."

Her skin pricked at his words. Sam deserved a childhood.

John cleared his throat. "The plan for the rest of us—Me,

Elijah, Trevor, and Robyn—is to get into the station, grab the others, then use the BMXs with the pegs to bring them back."

Robyn looked at John again. "Will we be fast enough with riders on the back?"

"We won't be able to outrun anyone who's on a mountain or road bike, if that's what you're wondering," Trevor said. "Counting on not having to. Calvin leads them away, Nate shows us how to get out undetected. We're relying on stealth here, not speed. It's the only way this works."

"If they're still alive when we get there." Nate's voice was flat. "There's a good chance we'll be too late and this whole thing's a waste of time."

Robyn shifted at his words and stared down at the table.

"Whether they're alive or not," John said, "the most challenging part will be getting in and out without being seen, so show me the map again."

They spent the next several hours going over the plan Nate drew up for them. The more they talked, the more she knew the truth: that despite his knowledge and experience, the odds were still stacked against them.

The first problem, of course, was the location. He explained to them how the station was huge and near the center of the city, and how the front half was surrounded at a distance by fire-ravaged buildings and a large empty space, which gave the lookouts ample warning if anyone unauthorized tried to approach it, especially if the night were clear. Approaching from the front really wasn't a possibility.

The other option—their only one, really—was through the concrete parking garage in the back. It rose up several levels above the ground, but the first floor had a direct entrance to the station, and it served as the Grims' fire exit.

According to Nate, there would be two men positioned at the onramp, one inside the parking garage at the door to the station, and another directly inside that door. They wouldn't be expecting anyone to attempt a rescue or attack. They were armed. And they were Grims. Nobody had tried anything like this before.

If there'd been electricity, this rescue would've been utterly impossible; video surveillance, walkie-talkies, and early warning alarms would've given the Grims eyes and ears everywhere. Now, the Members had to rely on their own eyesight and power of observation.

Besides getting past the guards, though, they would also somehow need to get close enough to the parking garage without being seen. While there were only four men devoted to watching the entrance itself, there was a constant rotation of foot and bike patrol that circled the area and watched for anything unusual. The best plan they could come up with was Calvin's diversion and dumb luck or, according to John, prayer.

"Same thing," Nate said.

Once inside, things would get messier. The halls were narrow and unpredictable. If any guns were fired, the sound would carry through the airy buildings and bring more company than they could handle. But they'd all be carrying. Even Calvin. Even John.

"Some things are necessary, no matter how tragic," was all John said.

If they made it out, John, Calvin, Trevor, and Robyn would take the others back on the foot pegs. They'd split up and, hopefully, all make it home. If someone wasn't back by daybreak, they'd evacuate their place and hope to find another location before the Members descended on them.

CHAPTER 14

When Elijah and Calvin finally retrieved the last of the bikes, it was dark enough to head out.

Sam, who had fallen asleep on the floor by the window, her cheek resting on the comic book, opened her eyes as the last one was wheeled across the floor. "What's happening?" she asked.

Robyn knelt beside her. "We're going to go get Danika's husband back from the people who took him."

"You're going, too?" she asked, and when Robyn nodded, she added, "Can I come?"

"You know you can't." She brushed a loose strand of hair from Sam's forehead. "It's crazy out there. I want you safe."

"So why are *you* going?" Sam sat up. "Why don't you stay here and wait with me? You said it's safe here."

"Safe for now. If we don't get Max back, I'm not sure it will stay safe." She was doing her best to explain. She didn't want to scare her, but Sam had to understand. "He can get us out of here. Can you imagine it?"

Sam was close to tears. "How do you know it will be any better? And you could die trying!"

"It's worth it. Making you safe is all that matters to me."

"If I mattered, you wouldn't go." Sam stood and Robyn scrambled to her feet. "You're leaving just like you did before when I woke up at Nate's, and you were gone, and I was so scared, and Nate and me had to get out so fast." She squeezed her eyes shut. "And we could hear their bikes and the shouting, and we walked and walked, and Nate's leg was hurting and I was so scared—and you were gone! And now you're trying to leave me again!"

Everything fell into place. That's why Sam had been so angry with her before. Nate had rescued her when her own sister had abandoned her. Only she hadn't, really. Robyn had been keeping her safe. And whether or not Sam could forgive her for it, that's what she had to keep doing for as long as she could. She steeled herself against emotion. The only thing she could do was go and hope she didn't die so Sam could have a chance to forgive her when she got back.

"Sam …" Robyn said.

Sam threw up her hands. "Fine," she said, staring out into the night.

"Samantha—"

"Just go." Her voice was little more than a whisper.

The boys were at the front door with the bikes. They'd checked the tires and chains. They were just waiting for her now.

"Love you." Robyn gently squeezed her sister's arm. Sam jerked away from her. "Don't ever forget it." It felt like goodbye. A final goodbye. She grabbed her bike and followed them out the door.

They started out, clinging as usual to the shadows from the buildings. It was already pretty dark, but their feet on the pedals and their tires on the pavement sounded like they were screaming their presence to everyone in the area. They traveled in a straight line, with Nate leading, then Trevor, Elijah, Calvin, and John. Robyn brought up the rear. It was slower than it would have been with Trevor leading, although she could tell Nate was trying to get them there as quickly as he could. But he was out of practice, and he'd never ridden with one leg before.

They traveled down a street she'd never seen, a back way that patrols avoided.

The cloud cover was helpful in making their group hard to see, but they knew they weren't completely invisible. They turned again, down a wider street, and continued to ride in the shadows. Robyn had no idea where they were, but she knew, without a doubt, that Nate did. Her breath caught in her throat as she heard the sound of at least two bikes approaching.

Nate slowed and coasted his bike in close to the nearest building. He unclipped his good foot clumsily and set it down as the bike stopped. The others pulled in behind him. All stood, barely breathing, as they listened to the sound of the bicycles approaching. Two riders slowly came towards them, talking to one another. All one of them would have to do was glance over at the building where the group stood and it would be over.

Looking up the line, Robyn saw Calvin, Elijah, and Trevor resting their hands on their pieces; Nate already had his drawn. The only one who hadn't pulled his hands from his handlebars was John, but his lips were moving. Probably praying. The two riders were almost there. They got closer, closer, closer … then passed by them in the dark.

After the riders' voices had faded in the night, Nate started up again, and the group followed. They continued into the next residential area and then up onto the grassy berm close to the city's perimeter. If they'd been up higher on the berm, closer to the crest, the ride would have been easier, but then they would have been silhouetted against the horizon. The cold, dry soil slid beneath their wheels.

"Watch out," Nate called from up ahead, his bike wavering as he controlled it with his one hand.

They slowed, riding along the berm and then down into the next suburbs. Soon, she could make out apartment buildings in the distance as they neared her neighborhood.

Without warning, Nate veered off their route and pulled into a narrow alleyway with just enough room for two across. They followed him until he stopped and signaled them to be quiet. Not that anyone was about to say anything. They were in the thick of the Grims' territory. Sure enough, footsteps echoed along the pavement. This time, there were several. There was nothing to hide behind and nowhere to go.

Nate held his fingers to his lips. The group at the end of the alley were clearly patrolling and sweeping the area. She held her breath, waiting for them to glance over, but they didn't. They kept walking.

"How?" Calvin whispered.

Nate was already shaking his head.

"Prayer, man," John said.

Robyn exhaled. It would be nice to be so certain about *anything*, never mind your creator.

They started out again, riding slower as Nate kept watch. *So close now.* She could just make out the shape of the station. They were almost to the street where the narrow pathway broke off, the one Nate had tried to show them before. She hoped he could still find it as easily as he thought he could because, if not, they were lost.

They turned down the final street, hugging the tall buildings, then turned into the tight path between two structures. The concrete multistorey parking garage was just ahead of them, across an empty street. Two guards, illuminated by the moonlight, stood at the bottom of the ramp, leaning on their handlebars.

"You're on," Nate whispered to Calvin. Elijah nodded.

"Don't waste this, guys." Calvin tore out of the shadows and rode straight towards the two guards. Before they could reach for their firearms, he flew past them, up into the dark of the garage. They jerked their bikes around and followed. She knew Calvin was leading them up through the levels of the winding interior ramps, away from the entrance, buying their small team some time. But the Grims would only chase the Independent for so long before giving up—or catching him. Either way, if they weren't completely out of there by then, it would be bad news for everyone.

"Let's go." Nate motioned them, and they coasted into the parking garage. The guard they'd been expecting by the door to the station was gone. "Joined the chase," Nate muttered. She wasn't sure, but he sounded worried. About Calvin? Had he started to care about what happened to them?

Of course, there would still be a Grim watching the door inside the station. The trick would be to take him out without alerting anyone else inside. The five remaining riders got off their bikes and stashed them tight against the wall. Tucked in close like that, they were almost completely invisible in the dark.

"I'm up," Nate said.

"Hey," Robyn whispered as he grabbed the silver door handle. He paused, and she suddenly had no idea what she was going to say. Finally, she said, "Be careful."

He nodded and pulled open the door, letting it close behind him. They were supposed to hang back and wait in case something went wrong but, instead, she stepped forward and placed her ear tight against the heavy door, listening. Of course, there was only silence. She would have heard a gunshot if there had been one, wouldn't she?

Please, be okay, she thought.

She stepped back at a sudden pressure on the door. Nate pushed it open and, surrounded by an eerie glow from inside, peered out at them. "You guys coming or what?" he asked.

They passed through the doorway into a long corridor. Robyn avoided looking down at the unconscious kid near the door.

Nate nodded to his right. "That's the way to the main entrance." He led the other way. "Guard shifts head in and out of it through two hallways. This is one of them. Let's be fast." She was bringing up the tail end again, but John stopped, letting her pass.

"You're unarmed," John said as she raised her eyebrows. "And I need to hide this guy. He'll bring us company faster than we're ready for it."

She continued past him, and she heard him open the door to the outside.

Robyn tried to be calm. The long hallway was lit by candles rigged along the upper edges of the wall; they cast long, eerie shadows. Everything was quiet, aside from their footsteps, which were too loud. John caught up as they rounded a corner. Robyn almost expected to see Members waiting for them, but it was empty.

Halfway down, Nate stopped. "This is it," he said, putting his hand on a door. "They'll be downstairs in a holding cell, guarded."

"No guns, remember?" Trevor said. "We don't want to bring

this whole place down on us."

Nate slowly pulled open the door. Robyn winced as it creaked, but all they heard from below was laughter. She was surprised at the stab of sympathy she felt for the people they were about to attack. They didn't realize they were about to have Nate crashing down on them. This time, John touched her shoulder, signaling her to let him go first. He was protecting her again. That or he knew she wasn't their best bet at getting in there.

Nate cautiously moved down the stairs, but it was more difficult for him to be silent with his limp. He landed hard on the third step and the voices stopped. The guards were clearly listening. A chair pushed backwards. They were coming. Just as a flash of black hair appeared at the base of the stairs, Nate leapt forward, followed by the rush of the other men. Robyn ran down afterwards but, by the time she got there, the two guards had been incapacitated. She didn't want to see. Trevor and the others had been quick and they'd had the advantage of surprise and, maybe, of expertise. Despite her best intentions, she glanced at the still bodies. The men on the floor were hardly men at all—boys, really. They most likely would have been juniors in high school, and now they were lying motionless. Playing cards were scattered on the table. She shouldn't care, but she let out her breath when she saw their chests rise and fall. Nate leaned over one and searched the pockets of one of the boys.

"Got it," Trevor said, leaning over the one closest the door. He held up a black lanyard with a large key hanging from it. "Let's go."

Elijah followed Nate and Trevor into the next room where the prisoners had to be. Robyn lingered behind, watching as John, tears running down his cheeks, crouched down beside one of the injured boys. It was strange to see him cry. His full beard and long hair, along with his imposing size, somehow made her think of some kind of strange cross between a superhero and Jesus.

"Do you know that one?" she asked.

He shook his head, not bothering to wipe his eyes. "No. But he's just a kid. They're all just kids." He looked towards the doorway where the men had gone to get Max and the others. "Our guys, too. All these kids running around trying to kill each other." He stood, shoulders slumped. "It must break His heart."

"John!" Trevor called. "We need you in here!"

John tore his eyes away from the guards and hurried into the next room. Robyn trailed after.

As soon as she entered the room, she was hit by a wall of stench: human waste, vomit, sweat, blood, who knew what else. She wretched, her stomach jerking up into her lungs. She hadn't eaten much of anything in the last few days, but she emptied what little food was in her onto the floor. Elijah, Calvin, and Trevor seemed to have recovered already, and John didn't react at all. He was instead wholly focused on the prisoners. Three men and a woman lay on the floor in the mess and their own blood. Trevor knelt in the wet beside the girl, leaning in towards her, speaking softly and touching her shoulder. He brushed dark strands from her face. *Stacie.*

"We're not going to be able to carry them out of here," Nate said, but John was already crouched low beside one of the men.

"Max," John said. "Max, wake up. Elijah, see to Bryant and Aaron." He pinched the man's shoulder, hard, and, after a short moment, Max slowly opened his eyes.

"John?" Max asked. His voice was muffled through his swollen jaw. He struggled to sit.

Elijah was now working to wake the two other men. Robyn

started as the girl suddenly shot up, screaming. She dragged herself away from Trevor into the corner of the room and pulled her legs in close, her eyes wide in panic.

"It's me." Trevor crouched down, extending his open palms to her. "It's just me. We're bringing you home, Stacie."

She stared for a moment, then threw herself into his arms. Sobbing, she clung to him as if he were keeping her from drowning.

The commotion had helped wake the others, it seemed. The three men struggled to get to their feet.

"What'd they do to you?" Elijah asked, but John reached out and put a hand on his arm in warning. They couldn't think about that now.

"Can you walk?" Trevor asked Stacie as they stood.

"I think so." Her voice shook. Robyn tried not to stare. The girl was around her age, maybe, or a few years older. She was a little taller, too. Her pale skin was smeared with blood. Whatever had happened to Stacie was their fault. Hers and Nate's.

Don't think about it now. Just. Don't. Think.

The men were on their feet, somewhat unsteady, but standing.

"I didn't want to tell them anything, John, but I did. I'm so sorry. I —" Long ashy hair hung down over his eyes. His cheeks were wet.

John waved his words away. "You did good, Aaron. You're alive. That's what matters. Let's get you out of here."

They made their way past the guards, up the stairs, and into the hallway that led back to the parking garage. They wouldn't have much longer before someone noticed the missing guard, or the shift change revealed the injured ones and the empty cell.

Nate, still leading, pulled open the door. No noise in the

parking garage or the street beyond.

The bikes were still there. Nobody had been back yet. Wordlessly, Nate struggled onto his bike. She picked up hers.

"Don't want to be a downer," Max said through clenched teeth. He was clearly in a lot of pain, and his ragged breath made Robyn figure his ribs were broken. "But how are we supposed to ride?"

"You're not," Trevor said, retrieving his BMX. He pointed to the foot pegs. "You ride with us."

"Ah. We're to be your human shields while they're shooting at us." Max grinned crookedly. "Sounds like a plan."

"Better than making you run home," Nate muttered as John and Elijah grabbed their bikes. "And, if it makes you feel better, I don't get a shield."

"What? I … can you even ride?" Stacie stared down at his hand and leg.

Robyn wished Nate could read her mind. *Give Stacie a pass. After everything the girl has been through. Please.*

"Ride?" Nate said. "I can barely walk. Blame your boy Trevor. He convinced me to get on this thing."

Robyn shot Nate a grateful look.

"Guilty." Trevor touched Stacie's hand. "And we're lucky he did. Now we all just need to make it back."

"You'll be with me," Robyn said to Stacie. Stacie glanced over at Trevor. Obviously, she'd thought she'd be riding with him. "You're smaller; I'm smaller."

"Right. Of course." Stacie climbed on and held onto Robyn's shoulders.

Bryant climbed on the back of Trevor's bike. Trevor's eyes were locked on Stacie.

"I'll keep her safe," Robyn said, as Aaron paired with Elijah and Max got on the back of John's bike. "Promise."

Nate glanced back at them before heading out. Their tires hummed against the pavement as they flew down the onramp towards the exit. The weight of their extra riders gave them downwards momentum, but it also made balancing trickier. The exit was just ahead; Robyn bore down, working with gravity, urging her bike onwards. Faster. *Faster.*

Nate, out first, led them. She almost thought they'd get away with it.

A shout rang out. She peered through the darkness. Two Members had just rounded the corner behind them. They'd been spotted.

Within seconds, the buzz of their tires picked up speed behind them. No way her group, doubled up on these bikes, could outrun these two.

She heard tires slide out in the dark behind them, someone colliding with pavement, and then a thud as the fallen rider hit a solid object—most likely a hydro pole. Good news. One down.

"Faster!" Stacie yelled into her ear.

Robyn gritted her teeth. Even in the cold, she was beginning to overheat. Sweat trickled down her forehead.

They turned down another street and then veered off onto another one.

Suddenly, in a flurry of motion, Nate's bike began to skid. With his feet still clipped into the pedals, he fell off his bike and slid across the pavement, pulling the bike with him.

"Keep going!" Bryant shouted at them. She knew why. The Grim behind them screeched to a halt. Clearly, he was willing to cut his losses and settle for Nate. The rest of them were in the clear.

Instantly, Trevor swung around so hard Bryant fell off the pegs. Robyn pulled her brakes, turning to watch. So did John.

"Trevor, stop!" Stacie called, but he didn't slow down, his bike angled directly towards the men.

The Grim let his bike fall as he stepped towards Nate. He reached into his jacket. Nate struggled from under the bike, but it was all happening too fast. Why did she suddenly feel like she couldn't breathe?

Trevor collided hard with the Grim as a gun fired. Robyn's ears rang as the bike slid out and the two men fell to the ground. The shooter's body lay motionless on top of Trevor's.

"Trev, No!" Nate freed his feet and shoved the bike off of his legs. He scrambled to his feet.

"No. No. No." He limped towards Trevor. Stacie hopped off the bike and ran to him too. Bikes clattered to the ground as the others crowded in, chase forgotten.

Frozen, Robyn watched them from where she stood with her bike. Inside, she echoed Nate's plea. *No. No. No. Please, God, no.*"

Nate pulled the Member off Trevor's body and knelt down beside him. He rolled Trevor over onto his back. "Please, Trev, get up." His voice cracked as he grabbed Trevor's bloodied shirt. "Please, just get up. Get up. Please."

Trevor didn't move.

CHAPTER 15

Trevor groaned and opened his eyes. Nate's breath caught in his throat. *He was alive.* Trevor frowned up at him and asked, "You okay?"

Air rushed into Nate's lungs again. "Are you shot?"

"Don't think so." Trevor sat up, unsteadily. He touched the back of his head. "Pretty sure I just knocked myself out when I hit the ground."

Nate pushed him, hard. "You idiot. You almost died. For *me.*"

"Would have been worth it." Trevor flashed a quick grin. It faded as he looked over at the fallen rider with … pity? Remorse? "But that guy … is he …"

John turned to look at the fallen Grim. He pulled open the coat, and then let it fall shut again. "Been shot," he said. There it was again, pity for the worst kind of people. "If I had to guess, I'd say he had his finger on the trigger as he was pulling out his piece. When Trevor ran into him, he squeezed it. Shot himself point-blank."

"I'm not going to waste my tears." Stephanie's voice was

hard, but Nate couldn't miss the relief in it. Relief like his. "Now let's get out of here before the others find us."

Trevor shakily got to his feet and moved to retrieve his bike. "I meant it, you know," he whispered to Nate. "It would have been so worth it."

"Nothing's worth dying for." Nate grabbed his own bike. *Especially not me.*

"Heaven's gotta be better than this place."

"Right," Nate said. "Heaven."

Trevor crouched by his bike, quickly working the chain back into place. "I mean it. I know where I'm going after this."

Nate imagined John nodding in the dark.

"God's got a plan, Coop. Thought you could use a little more time to see it." He stood and rolled his bike forward. It was ready to ride again. Swinging his leg over, he nodded. "But unless we all want to meet Him tonight, we need to get going. This place is going to be swarming with Grims."

John lingered, crouching by the wounded rider. "This boy's not gone. I'm just …"

Bryant spit on the ground but didn't say anything.

Fabric tore. Nate knew, without looking, that John was wrapping the wound.

"He's not worth it, Ashwood." *None of us are.*

"Everyone's worth it." John stood. "Now let's get out of here.

They headed out through the night again, retracing the route they used to get there. Nate was still shaken. Trevor had come back for him. After everything they'd gone through to rescue Trevor's own people, Trevor had risked it all for him. The sound of the bullet ringing out through the dark still echoed in his mind.

It was almost dawn. The night watch was heading in, and Nate knew the Grims would still be trying to figure out what happened. But his leg was killing him, and his good arm was almost exhausted with the effort of steadying his bike.

They turned onto their street just before daybreak. As they neared the house, Danika ran through the front door towards them with a shout. Max, on the back of John's bike, hopped off and caught her as she threw herself into his arms. He wrapped his arms around her.

Nate averted his eyes. He didn't need to see that. He slowed his bike to a near stop so he could pull his feet from the clips, then struggled off the bike. He limped with the bike up the path towards the house.

Calvin stood at the doorway, grinning. "Took you long enough." He came out to greet them.

"Knew you'd make it back, son," Elijah said, dismounting. The others had also arrived and were climbing off their bikes.

Calvin reached out for Nate's bike. "Here, let me help."

Nate let him take it. He'd have argued if he'd had any energy left, but he was using most of it to put one foot in front of the other. He wasn't sure if it was the ride or the fall, but he was done. He glanced over at Robyn. Her gaze followed Stacie and Trevor into the house. Was she jealous?

Nate left her to stash her bike with the others. All he wanted to do was get off his feet.

Inside, the light from the morning sun shone through the windows. This was as good a place as any. He leaned against the living room wall adjacent to the large window and then, a moment later, slid down it to sit. He pulled off John's cleated shoes.

Danika and Max walked by, his arm slung over her shoulder. They joined the others in the kitchen.

Nate turned his attention to his bad leg. He wouldn't be able to get any sleep later if he didn't do something about it now. He started at the calf, kneading it as hard as he could tolerate. He moved up above his knee, wincing as his fingers massaged the muscle.

"Hard ride?"

His fingers stilled at her voice. He didn't need to look up to know Robyn stood beside him. "I'm out of practice."

"I'm not, and I'm not feeling so hot either." She sat beside him, stretching her legs out.

He was surprised to feel her shoulder against his. "How's Sam?"

"Danika said she went to sleep in the bedroom just off the hallway as soon as we left. She's been sleeping all night. Must have been exhausted."

"No wonder, with everything. She'll be glad to see you when she wakes up."

"Yeah. She'll want to hear all about it. Pretty crazy, what Trevor did."

"Insane." He shook his head. "They're all insane here." He looked over to where John sat at the table, whispering with Max and the others. "John's filled their head with a bunch of religion and there's no room for rational thoughts."

"John took us in," she said quietly. "And saved their lives."

Nate shrugged. "Yeah, and Trevor saved mine. Nobody's saying they're not noble. I'm just saying they're not all there." He was watching them. "Still can't believe we made it back."

"Me neither. Sam would never have forgiven me if we hadn't."

"You'd die for her?" he asked. He knew the answer before she said it.

"'Course."

"I wouldn't."

"Nice." Her mouth twisted into a small grin. He knew she wasn't surprised at his response either.

"It's nothing personal. I wouldn't die for anyone."

"Not even Trevor?"

Trevor. He thought about it. *No. Not even Trev.* He shook his head again. "I love him like a brother. He's the only one who cares about me at all, and he's all I have left. But I'm not that person. Not that I'm scared of death. I'd just want it to be on my own terms."

Stacie laughed at the table, interrupting them. Laughed. Even after everything. He could see why Trevor allowed himself to feel hope for the future.

"What happened to your family?" Robyn asked, pulling her eyes away from the scene in the kitchen.

"Didn't have much of one to start with. Ran away when I joined the Grims, way before the blackout, way before life became this." He looked at his hands. Why was he telling her this? "Left after a bad night with my stepdad. This was his parting gift." He gestured to the long scar on his face. He forgot about it, most of the time. When he didn't, it reminded him of the night he failed the person who trusted him most. The night he'd left him behind.

"Trevor kept me updated." He forced himself to continue. She wanted to know him? Fine. "First winter after the blackout, my family all froze to death. Trev found them in the stupid little apartment. Survived the fires but too dumb to stay warm." His jaw tightened. "I didn't care about the folks. My mom and stepdad were a waste of space. But my stepbrother ..." He cleared his throat; tears started to form. He blinked them away. He should just stop now. He should just ...

"Your stepbrother?"

He forced the words out. "My stepbrother was eight. I felt bad about leaving him with them, but I couldn't make myself stay. He was such a sweet kid." He cleared his throat again. "Always thought I'd go back when I could and bring him to live with me."

She reached out and covered his hand with hers. He flinched at her touch, glancing over at her and then down at their hands. A rush of shame flooded him. She was sorry for him. For *him*. Did she figure his story meant he was human, that he was worth her pity? He didn't want it.

"I left him there," he said, his voice hard. She had to understand. "I knew what they were like, and I left him. And they let him freeze to death. That's on me." When she didn't pull her hand away, he added, "What happened to your folks? They were killed, right?"

He knew, of course, exactly what had happened to them. Sam had told him about it. She'd been so little at the time, but the memory had etched itself into her young mind. Robyn never talked about it, so Sam shared with Nate. He'd been waiting for a chance to use it, though he never thought he'd use it like this.

"Sam told you?" she said.

"Yeah. Grims? Could even have been me."

She abruptly pulled away her hand away. "Was it?"

He let the question hang in the air, heavy and ugly. It hadn't been him, but it could have been, just as easily. If he'd been there when it happened, the answer would be different.

"Don't know," he finally said. "Don't care. Things got crazy when the lights didn't come back on." He waited, then added, twisting his lips into a half smile, "Bet you're not so sorry for me now, are you?"

She stood, looking down into his eyes. He forced himself to meet her gaze.

"What's wrong with you?" she asked, her voice rising.

The conversation at the table beyond them stopped, and he felt their stares. He shrugged.

"You're an animal!" As she walked away from him, he let the smile slide off his lips. He blinked, his eyes burning. It was better for everyone if she remembered how she really felt about him.

"Sam?" Robyn called.

Nate struggled to his feet. The door to Sam's room was open, and Robyn was just coming out of another.

"Sam!" she called again.

Nate made his way down the hallway.

"Shhh." Danika came out of the remaining room. "Max is sleeping."

Robyn ignored her. "Sam!" She pushed past Danika, flinging open the door to Max's room.

"What's going on?" Max sat up.

"Sam!" Robyn said again. "Sam!"

"She was in her room," Danika started, and Robyn grabbed her arms, her fingernails digging into her wrists.

Nate's pulse pounded in his ears. The girl was gone.

"She's not there! Where's my sister?"

Danika's eyes went wide; Robyn released her and threw open the back door.

"Sam!" Robyn shouted into the street.

Nate knew Robyn wouldn't care if she was supposed to be keeping quiet and hidden. She wouldn't care if she gave them all away. Nothing mattered to her beyond her sister.

"Sam's missing?" Trevor asked, now in the hallway behind them.

"Samantha!" Robyn called again. She went back in to find Danika still staring into Sam's empty room.

"I saw her lay down," Danika said. "I saw her. She went to sleep."

"Then where is she?" John joined them in the room. The window was open, a cool breeze coming in. Danika wrapped her arms around herself, shaking her head. Anyone could have taken the sleeping girl, but who even knew she was here? Nate knew the answer even as he asked himself the question. Sam had run away.

"I'm going out to find her," Robyn strode past them to the front door.

"Wait!" Trevor said, grabbing her arm. "People are looking for you. You can't—"

"I don't care."

"You can't just go out there. The Grims, and now the other gangs, are hunting you. You know what they'll do to you if they catch you? Just slow down for a minute. Let's come up with some kind of plan. Let's …"

"Trevor, stop," John said. "We'll split up. We'll find her."

"Of course," Trevor said. He tightened his grip on her arm. "But let's figure out a plan first. We don't want to put everyone here at risk."

She blinked, startled, then laughed a short, harsh sound.

"You of all people?" Robyn asked, shaking her head at him. She jerked her arm away. "What happened to your big God?"

He opened his mouth to reply, but stopped as John stepped past him.

"Stacie, you stay here and watch for Sam. She might make her way back. Trevor and I'll take the streets on the north," John said. "We'll ask around, see if anyone's seen her. We have several hours of good daylight left. Let's not waste them."

Trevor didn't argue this time.

John added, "Elijah and Aaron, you take the west streets from here to Kenzing Ave. Bryant and Calvin, west from Kenzing to Barton."

"We'll canvas the south side as far as daylight will let us," Max said, leaning against Danika, his fingers entwined with hers. "Maybe someone saw where she was headed."

"Nate, you go east with Robyn."

"I don't need Nate with me," Robyn said. "I'll go alone."

Nate didn't say anything. He wanted to find Samantha. But a little girl out there on her own? There were so many things that could have happened to her by now. Besides, what kind of help would he be to Robyn? He'd just slow her down.

He limped back to the living room and sat down. What better way to prove to her what kind of man he was?

As the house emptied and the others retreated again into the kitchen, Nate sat in the silent room and stared at his hands, trying to ignore the hollow feeling in his chest.

CHAPTER 16

"Sam!" Robyn called, her voice echoing through the empty streets. "Sam!"

She stopped at one of the first houses and banged on the door. There was movement inside, but nobody came out. She pounded hard, again. Finally, she pushed it open. A woman cowered against the wall, holding a small, pale boy.

"Have you seen a little girl; she's about six?" Robyn asked. The woman shook her head. "Are you sure?"

"We haven't," the boy said. "We never go out."

She studied them. They weren't lying. She banged the door shut behind her.

At the next door, her second knock was answered by a thin old man in a long brown housecoat. He stared off to somewhere past her as she asked her questions. He didn't say a thing.

I don't have time for this. If he wasn't going to answer her, she'd need to look for herself. She pushed her way past him into the house, peering into the rooms. He followed her, ghost-like. The house smelled of death. Sam wasn't there.

At the third house, another man answered the door, but

a young woman edged him out of the doorway after Robyn's questions started. They insisted they hadn't seen her sister, and that, if she didn't leave them alone, she'd regret it.

"You'll bring the Members down on us, with all your shouting," the woman said before slamming the door.

The next houses were all the same and, although some were abandoned, most housed people who would tell her nothing. She knew she was being reckless. People could easily be armed, or someone bigger and stronger than her could put a quick end to her search. She kept going, though, house by house, letting herself in if nobody answered the door. Every face seemed to hold a lie, a secret.

"Sam!" she called, between each doorstep and as she crossed over into the next street. The sound of tires approached behind her, but she couldn't stop to look. She had one mission. Just one. Find Sam. She ran up to the next house and banged on the door so hard the palm of her hand stung.

"What's going on?" She turned to see the blue bandana on the head of a portly teenager, his hand resting on his sidearm.

"I'm looking for my sister. She's out here somewhere on her own."

She waited for him to show something: sympathy, maybe, or concern. Or suspicion of her. Instead, his face remained dull and passive as he eased his hand from his gun.

"What're you hoping to accomplish out here?" he asked, leaning on his handlebars.

"I'm going to find her."

He snorted. "Really."

It wasn't a question, but she didn't care. She didn't have time for this.

"Well, keep it down," he said after a moment of silence.

"You don't want to get people worked up." When she said nothing, he straightened up. "No more noise from you, got it?"

She nodded. *As if.*

He huffed, getting back on his ride. "See that you do," he said as he pulled away. She waited until he disappeared around the corner before forcing her way into the next home.

House after house after house revealed nothing. No Samantha. No witnesses. No leads. Were the others any luckier? They were all out there looking. All except Nate, but what else should she have expected from him? It wasn't like he'd ever claimed to care about her or Sam.

Unlike Trevor.

Trevor, who was all in when it came to his friends. *But Sam goes missing, and he wants to wait. To plan. To let whatever chance we have to find her slip away.* She shook the thought away. Trevor believed in the greater good. Always had. Sam just wasn't the greater good to him. She wasn't his family. And he wasn't theirs. She'd known it that moment in the park after giving the Grims the slip, when Trevor had held her close—and she'd felt no safer than she had before she'd known he was there. Trevor didn't make her feel safe. Not like Nate.

Nate. But Nate was a Grim, and the Grims were the reason she was running. They'd killed Meri. They'd killed her parents.

She pushed Nate's face from her mind. All that mattered was her sister. And she was running out of time.

***

The sun was low on the horizon by the time she snaked her way through the streets and was nearing the house again. She was less than a block away, one street over, from where she'd started. She'd tried to hit as many places as she could, but her path had been messy, haphazard. She was sure she'd missed some.

How are the others doing?

She was losing the light, and her sister was out there somewhere. She had to be okay. *But what if she's not?* She tried to force the thought away like she'd been doing all day, but it refused to disappear. *What if she's not?*

"If she's not, I'd know it," she whispered. *I'd feel it.*

At fifteen, Robyn took a pretty bad fall during one of her downhill bike races. She'd hit one of the jagged rocks and, instead of recovering from the jolt, she'd instinctively hit her front brake and flipped over her handlebars. She'd fallen off the edge of the dirt path into the brush in the ditch below. She'd been knocked unconscious and awoke to the sound of her parents calling her name. When she'd opened her eyes, her mom was pushing back the branches and leaves and then kneeling down in the grass beside her.

"I knew you would be okay," her mother had said at the time, and Robyn, even now, could hear her voice as clearly as she had then. "If you hadn't been, I would have felt it."

Robyn had to believe it was the same for Sam. Her sister was all she had left. "Sam!" She took a moment to catch her breath to call again. "Sam!"

"Robyn?" It was a tiny voice from somewhere in the darkness, so quiet she could have imagined it.

"Samantha?" She peered into the darkening street. Silence again. Only silence. "Samantha!"

"Robyn." Quiet, but real. Had to be real. She crossed the lawn of the house nearest her, peering into the black windows, looking for any sign her sister had been there. The side door was ajar, hanging crookedly off its hinges. Was she inside?

"Sam, you here?"

"Robyn." It was still soft, but this time, she could hear it clearly. She raced past the front door to the side of the house. Scattered debris and dark shadows cast by the house made it hard to see anything.

"Robyn?" Her sister called again. This time, the voice was quiet but closer. She followed it to the backyard. It was a mess of overgrown grass and tall weeds. "Where are you?"

"Down here."

Down... where? Robyn's eyes combed the ground. What if Sam were pinned underneath something, hidden by the grass? She looked for a fallen tree or something else that could be covering her sister. After another step, she saw it. The earth seemed to rise up slightly and then disappear into blackness. It took seconds for Robyn to reach the jagged opening of the storm cellar. Falling to her knees, she peered through, down into the space below. It was pitch black.

"Are you okay Sam?"

"I—I'm sorry." Sam's voice, though closer now, was still barely audible. "I didn't see..."

"It's okay. I'm going to get you out." The flat, square door, worn through by the weather or neglect, must have broken when Sam walked over top of it. Robyn looked for a ladder. Nothing. There had to be something she could use to get her out.

"Can you see anything?" The cellar opening had clearly been too small to have a full-sized exterior staircase. Maybe the ladder was still down there.

"Too dark."

"Can you feel around for a ladder. Or..." An idea struck her. "Or another door? It could open to the main house from inside." When Sam didn't answer, she called again, "Are you okay? Sam!"

"Think so. Can't get up. And I'm tired."

"Are you hurt?" She didn't reply. "Sam! Sam!" She shouted her sister's name, as loud as she could. Somewhere in the back of her mind, she knew she was drawing attention to herself, knew anyone could hear her and find her. But she didn't care. Not even a little. "Sam, can you hear me? Sam!"

Robyn scrambled to her feet. Why wasn't Sam answering anymore? What if… she didn't finish the thought. She sprinted to the side door again and into the house. There was still enough light coming through the open windows to see the stairs to the basement. She took them two at a time, descending into the darkness. She didn't know if anyone lived there, but it didn't matter.

"Sam!" She called. No reply. "Can you hear me?" She found the wall nearest her and, running her hand along it, followed it into another room. She felt her way into a small empty closet, and then back out again. She fought against panic as she followed the walls with her hand until she reached the stairway. No interior access. *What do I do? What do I do?*

At the top of the stairway again, she looked around the empty room and through the open doorway into the next. The place had been cleaned out—they'd left nothing she could use to get her sister out. Her only other option was to lower herself down into the cellar, try to land as carefully as she could, hope she didn't land on top of Sam. If there wasn't a ladder down there, maybe there'd be shelves or something she could use to climb back up. She darted out the door and slammed into the chest of a person standing there.

Nate put a steadying hand on her arm.

"Nate! What are you—"

"I could hear you calling her. Took me less than five minutes to find you. You're making way too much noise. Gonna bring everyone serious trouble if you keep it up."

She looked up into his face.

His hand was still on her arm. "Getting yourself killed isn't going to help her."

"Nate, she's *here*." She shook him off. "Down here." She jogged around to the back of the house. She could hear his uneven gait hurrying after her. She knelt down again. "Sam!"

Again, there was no reply. Nate peered over her shoulder.

"She was answering me before." She could hear the tears in her own voice. *Steady. Be steady for Sam.* "I'm worried about the cold and if she's hurt from the fall. She was so quiet before, and now …"

"Okay." He cut her off, limping to the edge of the opening. "Okay. Any idea how deep it is?"

"I don't know. How deep are storm cellars usually? Seven, eight feet? I was thinking there might be something down there that we could use to climb up, if I went in after her."

"I'm taller than you. It would make sense for me to go." Robyn was already shaking her head. He added, "The hand's not a problem."

"It's not that. Whoever goes down to get her—if there' s no ladder down there—is going to need help getting out. Nate, you need to stay up here to pull us out."

"You don't know what's down there."

"Sam's down there."

He hesitated only a moment. "Fine."

"Fine."

Without another word, Nate lay flat on his stomach beside her, bracing himself with his weak arm. She lowered herself, feet first, through the opening in the hatch, her legs hanging down into the darkness. "Lower me as far as you can. I don't want to hurt Sam if I land on her."

"Will do my best."

With one more deep breath, she shimmied off the edge, lowering her body into the space below. She held tight to the ledge for a moment until she felt Nate's hand grasp hers. He was ready for her.

She forced herself to let go and then she clutched Nate's hand with both of hers. She allowed him to lower her down.

It was so dark. How close was she to the bottom?

"Oh—" Nate's voice warned before she felt his fingers slip. Her feet instantly touched the floor. She felt a slight cushioning beneath her. An entrance mat.

"Sorry. You okay?" Nate called down to her.

"Yeah." She waited for her eyes to adjust, but there was so little light from above that they just weren't. "Sam?" she called in a whisper. When there was no reply, she called again, louder, "Sam!" Relief washed over her when she heard someone stir to her right. "Sam!"

"Robyn?" The voice was muffled and slurred but unmistakably Sam's.

"I'm here, Sam. We're getting you out." Dropping to her knees, Robyn felt her way to her sister. "Can you sit up?" She felt for her sister's hand. It was cold.

"I think so." She felt her sister struggle up. "Knew ... find me."

"Of course. Of course I did." Robyn slid her hands along her sister's body, feeling for injury, for broken bones or blood. "You need to tell me if you're hurt."

"My leg hurts." Sam sounded so tired. She was still shivering, though, which meant they weren't too late.

"Found anything you can use to get back up here?" Nate called down.

"Looking." Robyn squeezed her sister's hand. "We're going

to get you out of here as fast as we can. But I need to see if there's something we can use to climb up, okay?"

"Don't leave me." Sam whispered. She eased back to lie down again. "Too dark."

"I'm not leaving. Promise." She wasn't sure Sam heard her.

Robyn felt her way back through the dark until she reached the flat wall. She stood and traced her way along it until she came to smooth wood, jutting out. Shelves. She rattled them. They were firmly attached to the wall. There was no way to move them and use them as a ladder. She felt inside the closest shelf, knocking over some sort of canister and brushing her fingertips along what felt like cans and small boxes. The shelves were stocked, but how was she supposed to use any of these supplies to get them out? Whoever left this stuff in here wouldn't be back for it. They must have taken the ladder with them when they sealed the cellar to prevent looters.

She felt what little hope she'd been clinging to evaporate. There must not be another exit, not if nobody had found it before now. Nate was going to need to go for help.

"Nate!" There was silence above her. She tried again. "Nate, quit messing around."

She squinted up at the opening. He wasn't there. *He wasn't there!*

A scraping noise filled the room, and she whipped around to find the source. Something shifted at the far end of the room.

"My Grandma used to have a storm cellar like this. Had two exits. Figured there must be another one here, too." Nate's voice reached out to her from the dark. "Found a latch at the top of the closet wall."

The familiar clink of Nate's lighter was followed by the click of the flint wheel and a small flame, lighting the space around him. "She okay?"

Robyn shook off the image of Nate as some sort of angel, standing illuminated in the dim light. "Think so. She's freezing though." She knelt down beside Sam.

Nate came farther into the room. He couched down beside them. "Here." He handed her his lighter. She raised her eyebrows when he straightened up and pulled his hoodie off over his head. "We need to get her as warm as possible. We don't know how long she's been down here." He wrapped the hoodie around Sam's body as well as he could. Robyn tried not to notice Nate start to shiver. His thin t-shirt wasn't doing much against the cold. "I think we need to get her out as soon as we can. That hoodie won't be good enough."

She nodded and handed him back his lighter, then lifted Sam as gently as possible.

"I can …"

"I got her." She waited for Nate to lead the way up the stairs.

Outside, there was enough light to see the street, and she passed Nate, her small charge cradled in her arms. She nearly ran the half block back to the house. Nate kept up behind her.

As she jogged up the walk, Stacie opened the front door. "What happened?"

"Sam fell though a storm cellar door. I don't know how bad she's hurt. Maybe we shouldn't have moved her, but she was so cold." Robyn tried to blink away her tears but it was useless. There were too many and they dripped off her chin. "She's drifting in and out."

"Let's get her in that first bedroom and warm her up, quick as we can. We can check for other injuries." Robyn followed Stacie down the hall, leaving Nate standing alone in the dark.

CHAPTER 17

Stacie had them. They'd be okay; he knew it. He stared down the empty hallway. Why had he gone after her? He answered his own question; she would have brought the whole neighborhood down on them with her shouting. He scuffed the dry floor with his shoe, thinking about the panic in her voice. He turned away. They'd call if they needed him.

He limped towards the front door and peered out. Everything was quiet now. The other riders were still out there, looking for Sam. They'd be back soon enough.

But he had time.

He rubbed his leg. A block and a half back to the storm cellar. He'd only caught a glimpse, but what he'd seen had been promising. He hadn't been able to identify the specific contents in the dark room, but he was able to make out cans and boxes lining the shelves. What would be stocked in a storm cellar?

Food. There'd be food. But there might be other things too: blankets, tools, weapons. *Things worth something to a Member.*

There was no way he'd convince any Member to let the three of them out of the city; the risk was just too much. But maybe—

maybe—he could find a Grim who had been friendly with him before or had some sort of chip about Marshall's leadership. Then, maybe, he could negotiate a way out for himself. If he had the right things to trade and the right person to trade with.

Whatever plan Ashwood or Max Vargas or whoever thought they had, what were the chances of it actually working—with a cripple and an injured kid?

Make a deal for yourself. He gripped the doorframe until the wood bit into his hand. How long did he have until Robyn thought to tell the others about the supplies down there? He could go there, take what he needed, find someone to make a deal with—maybe even before they realized he'd gone. This was his chance. His one, solid chance.

He stepped back into the house at the whir of approaching tires. John was leading the way, followed by Trev. He went out to meet them on the lawn.

"She back?" John was breathless as he slowed his bike to a stop.

Nate nodded.

"Is she okay?"

"So far, I think."

"Thank you, Lord. Trevor, let's round up everybody who's still looking, let them know she's back. You go west for Elijah and the others. I'll head out to find Max and Danika. Thanks, Nate."

Nate sighed deeply. *Can't do it.* "John, we also found a cellar full of supplies. I'll give you directions to it when you get back."

"Good man."

Nate felt the weight of his words as John disappeared on his bike. *Good man.*

More like dead man.

***

"You awake?" Nate opened his eyes at Robyn's voice, drifting through the dark house.

He blinked up at her face in the dawn light. "Am now." He sat up, stiff from sleeping on the living room floor. The others had spent a good part of the night gathering the supplies from the cellar, and, aside from Max and Danika who'd retired to one of the bedrooms, were now sleeping on the floor around him. He leaned against the nearby wall.

Robyn sat beside him. "She's going to be okay, you know."

"Good."

"Stacie says hypothermia, but we caught it in time. We spent the night warming her up. Stacie's still in with her now."

"How's the leg?"

"We don't know for sure yet, but Stacie doesn't think it's broken. Maybe the mat cushioned her landing. Even if it's not broken, though, Sam's in pain."

"She awake now?"

"No. Sleeping. But she was awake at night a little. Thanks for coming for us, Nate."

"I told you, I didn't want you to bring the whole neighborhood down on us."

"Still …"

"Listen, if I hadn't been there, you would have found another way."

"Maybe. Maybe not. All I know is we were lucky you were there." She shifted and her shoulder brushed his. "You're freezing!"

"I'm okay." He *was* freezing. He hadn't retrieved his hoodie from Sam.

"And you're bleeding!"

He followed her gaze to the shallow scratches down his

forearms. "From the cellar door. They're not deep. Really." He met her eyes. She cared. *I don't want her to care. Do I?*

"Does it hurt?"

He shook his head. "Nah."

She glanced away from him, around the room. "I'm surprised everyone's still sleeping."

"Yeah, I told them about the cellar when they all got in last night. They managed to clean it out before anyone else could find it."

"What all was in there?"

"Emergency supplies. Canned food mostly, some of it still good. Whoever it belonged to never got a chance to use it."

"You remembered where to find it?"

He tapped his head. "Good for something."

"Right." She leaned back against the wall and sighed deeply. "Know what I bet finding those supplies means?"

"No. What?"'

She allowed herself a small smile. "Breakfast."

***

Nate watched Danika and Sam lying on the floor by the window from the kitchen. The light from the afternoon sun shone on them. They were reading the comic he'd given Sam.

It had only been three days, but it felt longer. Sam's ankle was sprained, at the very least. Their best guess was that, while that entrance mat had been able to absorb some of the impact when she landed, she'd rolled her ankle. It was impossible to know for sure without an X-Ray, but the swelling had already started to go down and the pain was ebbing. The cold water from the outside made a decent cold compress.

Still, Stacie didn't want Sam to put any weight on it for the next several days; even after that, she should take it easy. But the

Grims had to be closing in; between Robyn's noise and the intel from Aaron and the others, it was only a matter of time.

Escape before had been a long shot; now, it was impossible.

They planned anyway. Stacie stood at the counter and sorted the few medical supplies they had. Robyn, Trevor, Max, John, and Aaron gathered with Nate around the kitchen table, memorizing the pattern of the northeast perimeter guard rotation Max showed them.

"I can't give you exact times, obviously," Max said, "but there's always a lag between the time one team passes this point" —he tapped the little circled bridge on the map— "and the time the other team gets there." He looked around the table. "There will be no room for error. There are some bushes several feet away from the bridge where we'll wait. It's a tiny space of time, and you'll need to rush the bridge. You'll have seconds." He glanced over at Aaron.

"Trevor's coming with you, all the way to the garrison. And I'm coming too," Aaron said. "Normally, we'd escort you to the bridge, and then you'd need to make it the rest of the way on your own. But it's pretty complicated, and with an injured kid and …" his gaze glanced off Nate's hand. "… an injured rider, you'll need extra help to get the rest of the way. Trevor has worked with Max long enough to have the route memorized by now, but I know it, too. My grandpa's farm was one of the first ones they garrisoned. I'll take you."

"We'll miss you here," John said. "You're an integral part of this team and I've been blessed to have you working by my side." The way he said it made Nate wonder if Aaron was so ashamed of surrendering the information to the Grims that he was leaving. John seemed to be telling Aaron he had nothing to be sorry for. Nate knew the Grims. John was right.

Aaron nodded.

"You, too, Trevor," John said.

"You'll need to get out of sight as fast as you can," Max said. "You guys get across that bridge, and John and I will disappear before the guards even know anything's up."

"That's the plan, anyway," John said, his smile back in place. "God willing, right?"

"You're really coming, Trev?" Nate asked. Not that he was complaining, but Trevor had seemed pretty set on working in the city. On making things different for the people.

"Not giving up on this place," Trevor said. "But how can I keep you safe if I'm in here and you're out there somewhere? We're family, man."

"Anyone coming with you?" Nate asked, glancing over again at Stacie. She'd never told them about her time with the Grims, but he knew she'd told Trevor. Nate knew what his gang was capable of.

Trevor shook his head. "Stacie says she wants to stay to make a difference." She looked up and met his eyes. "Maybe we'll meet again when things are better."

Nate shook his head. "Good luck with that." He glanced at Robyn. He didn't know what he expected to see. Relief, maybe, that Stacie wasn't coming with Trevor. But her eyes were trained on John.

"When do we leave?" she asked.

"As soon as it's dark enough," John said.

"And you're sure Sam will be okay on the handlebars?"

"We'll go as slow as possible, stick to the shadows and brush where possible, and pray like crazy."

Impossible. Nate didn't say it out loud. They all knew the odds were slim at best. They didn't really have a choice. There was no way Sam could balance on foot pegs all that way on one leg, not with a sprained ankle. Riding the handlebars, leaning against the cyclist—would be her best shot.

"And you're really giving me the fixie and the cleated shoes?" Nate asked John for the third time that day.

"Really giving you them."

"Thanks. Appreciate it." He was grateful to John for a lot more than shoes, but the shoes seemed the simplest.

They all stared at the map for a moment more.

"You guys need to sleep," Max said, finally looking back up at them. "It's going to be a long, crazy night and you need to rest up before you go."

"It's broad daylight," Nate said. "I'm not a vampire."

"You need to sleep," Max said. "No mistakes tonight."

"Fine." He guessed it beat the alternative, which was standing around and waiting or making small talk with the rest of them. He glanced at Robyn again. It was best they didn't talk anyway. He'd been trying to fool himself before, back when he'd pretended she was just a loose end. Now, denying the way he felt about her was almost impossible, but admitting it to her—or to himself—wouldn't do either of them any good. Robyn wasn't the type of girl who would ever forget he'd been a Grim, and he'd never deserve her even if she could. Instead, he crossed the room to Sam and Danika. He joined them on the floor by the window, lying on his side with his head propped up on his palm so he could watch them read. Danika tolerated him, now that Max and the kid were both back.

He listened for a couple pages. He couldn't remember anyone reading to him. But here it was, the whole world falling apart, and Sam had a real shot at a childhood. He stole a quick look at Danika's slightly rounded belly, the fabric of her shirt pulled tight. Maybe her kid did too, even in this place. Its parents would be tough. They'd protect it. And it would be loved, at least. He didn't used to think that mattered. Now …

"Max says we're supposed to sleep." Nate quietly interrupted Danika's reading.

Danika raised her eyebrows at him but let Sam handle it.

"Can we finish this chapter?" Sam asked. "Please, Nate?"

He stifled a yawn. "Okay. Then you need to head to your room with your sister. I'll come wake you guys when it's time." Nate had taken to sleeping out in the living room on the floor with the other single men. He rolled onto his back, closed his eyes, and listened to Danika's voice as she finished the page.

***

Robyn leaned against the doorframe between the kitchen and the living room. Her sister seemed almost happy. Hopeful, maybe. She had Nate to thank for that. He was barely even talking to her now. Maybe he'd start again when they reached the garrison. *If* they reached the garrison.

"I'm going to pack up some supplies," John told her. "Trevor, you and Max should wrap it up. You need to sleep, too."

"Right," Trevor said from behind her, pausing in his conversation with Max. "I'll be joining Nate in a bit. Just going over last-minute details again." Of course he was. He wanted to make sure he did it right, that he kept everyone as safe as possible.

She studied Nate, who was asleep on the floor. The setting sun illuminated his gaunt cheeks and the long scar on the side of his face. He'd gotten his hoodie back. Dirty and disheveled like everybody's, it clung to his thin frame, rising and falling as he breathed. It was the strangest thing, knowing she could count on him.

She watched John walk down the dark hallway. After a moment, she hurried after him.

"Hey, can I help you pack?" she asked as he opened the door to the room with the bikes. Backpacks from the other house were inside. He picked one up and put it on the bed.

"I'm okay," John said. "This shouldn't take too long. Just filling a couple of packs for you guys to take with you."

"I'd like to help anyway."

John shrugged. "I never turn down help. Mind grabbing those three packs, then?" He pointed out the three backpacks nearest the door.

Robyn carried them over to him and set them down beside the other one.

"Color preference?" he asked as he dumped the contents of the bags out onto the bed. There were canned goods, bandages, and half-full water bottles, as well as a small pair of purple mini gloves.

She picked them up, turning them over in her hands.

"One of the Independents got those gloves as a trade on a job," he said. "Donated them for a rainy day. This must have been the day he was thinking of." He smiled. "Bet they would fit Sam perfectly."

She looked up at John, the soft gloves still in her hands. "Why are you helping us?"

He started sorting the cans and supplies on the bed. "Why not?" he asked, clearly dodging the question. It wasn't good enough for her, so she waited.

Finally, he sighed. "It's what I'm here for. 'Whatever you do for the least of these, you do for me,' you know?"

She really didn't, but she nodded anyway. It sounded Biblical enough that she didn't push it.

"Anyway, God saved me, so I'm trying to be His hands and feet here while I can."

The hands and feet of God. He was serious. She helped him finish separating the goods and arranging them in a line along the edge of the bed.

"Okay, so let's start by picking three cans for each pack," he said.

"That's a lot, even with the extra from the cellar."

"It's fine," he said. "We've got much more than when we started. We'll be fine."

She laid down the gloves and looked over the food. She would have refused it if not for the idea of Sam going hungrier than she had to.

Robyn slowly scanned the choices, taking longer than she needed to. "John?" she finally said, clearing her throat. "You said that nobody was good. Before, when you first sat down with Nate and me."

"Mm hmm." He was choosing the medical supplies, not looking at her.

"But you still think He, like, loves you and stuff?" She fiddled with the edge of a can now.

"Mm hmm. Know He does."

"But what if you did something really horrible? Unforgivable?" She didn't even know why she was asking him.

"Are you asking for Nate?" John had stopped working and was studying her face.

Of course he thought she was asking for Nate.

"No," she said. The truth was burning her. She had to tell someone. Someone good. Someone who could absolve her. Or condemn her. Or something. "The Independent wasn't dead when I took his bike. I took it and just left him there." She waited for his reaction, holding her breath. He didn't seem particularly surprised; he simply nodded once. "I didn't think I could help him anyway. But maybe I could have. They hurt the guy after I left with his bike. I know he died in a lot of pain. That's on me."

John nodded again. She wasn't sure what she was hoping for. He was quiet for what felt like a long time, turning his attention back to sorting supplies.

"Robyn," he finally said, "I'm just a man. I can't tell you what would have happened if you'd helped him, or what you should have or could have done. If you've been feeling guilty, it's because you already know the answer."

Tears pricked her eyes.

"But that's the thing about my God. We don't have to deserve His love." He tapped his palm against his chest. "I know I don't. He loves me anyway. And that's the thing about love. When you love someone—really love them—nothing is too big to forgive."

They both jumped as the door swung open and Nate leaned in. "Sam's ready for bed now. You should sleep, too." He hesitated. "You guys look intense. Did I interrupt something?"

"No," Robyn said quickly. "Thanks again, John, for everything." She hurried past Nate, brushing away the moisture in her eyes before joining Samantha in the chilly room.

"Hey," Sam said from under the thin blankets.

"Hey to you," Robyn said, crawling in with her. She wrapped her sister in her arms, warming them both.

"Nate says we're leaving tonight."

"That's what I'm told."

"I'm pretty scared."

Me too. "Everything will work out. You'll see."

"Night."

"Night."

Robyn closed her eyes against the bright sun shining down

on them through the window. For all the light it offered, she could have used more heat. Tonight would be worse. She thought of the purple gloves that would warm Sam's hands later, and the quiet assurance John had of this great forgiveness. She lay in the bright room, willing herself to stop thinking and just sleep but, instead, all she could do was replay John's words in her mind. *When you love someone, nothing is too big to forgive.* She knew things couldn't be as simple as he thought they were. Of course she knew it. But part of her whispered, *But what if they are?*

***

"Wake up, sleeping beauties." Nate's voice close to Robyn's ear brought her world quickly back into focus as she woke. She'd found sleep after all.

It was dark already, the room an inky black. Nate held his lighter out, casting a yellow glow on his face. "Everyone's ready to go."

"Why didn't you wake me sooner?" She threw the covers off her but left Sam covered. The air was frigid and her skin prickled with the chill.

"We thought we'd give you and the kid as much time to sleep as we could. And you're welcome."

"Is it time?" Sam asked from beside her, slowly sitting up.

"You betcha," Nate replied.

"It's so dark."

"Moon's mostly hiding tonight. That's a good thing. Makes it harder for the bad guys to see us."

"Harder for us to see where we're going, too," Sam said.

Robyn stood. She gently gathered her sister up in her arms.

"Very true," Nate said, his voice still carefree. "Luckily, Max knows the way. We'll just have to follow close."

"What if it's too dark?" Sam asked.

"We'll hope it won't be. He'll signal us if he can't see the way up ahead." Nate whistled softly to demonstrate.

Robyn knew how black the night could get if the cloud cover was too thick. When they reached the others, she tried to keep her voice from betraying her fear. "Why aren't we just waiting until a brighter night?"

"It's better like this," Max said. "The less light they have to see us, the better. We couldn't have chosen a better night. Trust me."

"I'm trying," she said.

"We're taking the mountain bikes. Better traction in the park once we're outside the city." John turned to Sam. "Sam, Aaron's going to be giving you a ride on his handlebars. You just lean back against his chest. It's going to feel a little bumpy. Think you can be brave?"

"Yes."

"Good girl. And look, these will help your fingers stay warm, even if the ride seems long." He handed Sam the gloves, and Nate brought his lighter closer to them so she could see their bright purple hue.

"They're beautiful," she whispered and slid them on. She held up her hands, turning them over in the glow of his lighter, admiring her gloved fingers. Then she looked up at John. "I'm ready now."

Nate shoved his lighter back into his jeans.

As they opened the front door, a burst of cold air hit them. Tears sprung up in Robyn's eyes. Beside her, Sam winced, visibly bracing herself against the cold. They listened, waiting for their eyes to adjust to the dark. They had to be able to see the terrain or they'd never make it out. Aaron mounted his bike and held the handlebars steady. Robyn lifted Sam up and helped her get as comfortable as possible.

Then Robyn mounted her bike, along with the others. "We need to be quiet and precise," Max said. "Go as fast as possible, but remember we have Sam up on the bars, and Nate on the fixie. We obviously won't be able to see much, so follow close. You'll hear my signal if it gets too dark to continue. One whistle to stop, two to go. But you need to trust me. Remember, no room for error."

The silence seemed to be affirmation because he didn't repeat his instructions.

With Max leading the way, Nate, their slowest rider, followed close behind. Max said he'd listen for Nate and make sure not to go too fast. Aaron, with Sam, followed behind Nate, then Robyn, followed by Trevor and John. She knew the last rider was always at the most risk; if someone heard them, or they drew attention to themselves as they passed a Member, he'd be the last one out of danger. Was John thinking about his wife and little boy right now, out there beyond the city boundaries somewhere? How did his wife feel about her husband risking his life, night after night, for a bunch of people he didn't even really know? How could he force himself to go on without them? She could tell it hurt him to be away from them, but he did it anyway.

Hands and feet of God, he'd said.

Max veered off the street, cutting between two houses and then between two more. They snaked their way through the neighborhood to the outskirts where the blackout had interrupted the new development and left it half-finished and unpaved.

Robyn tried to picture the map Max had worked so hard at getting them to memorize. She tried to match the penciled images to the route she now rode near-blind. Nate would have had no trouble with it, but it was already fuzzy to her. How much longer did they have?

Her fingers ached with the cold and the wind burned her eyes. She blinked, trying to clear them. They'd started watering just after setting out, and now, with the bikes kicking dirt and sand up into the air, everything was a blur.

"Hold up a second," Trevor quietly called from behind her, breaking the silence rule.

She wasn't the only one having some trouble. The group slowed to a stop. Aaron, in front of her, wiped one palm on his pant leg and then wiped his face. It was too dark to make out Max and Nate, but she assumed they were doing the same. She glanced behind at Trevor. He knelt by his bike.

"Chain issues," he said. "I think there's something caught in it."

"What happened to whistling?" she asked Trevor while he fiddled with bike, trying to distract herself.

"That's Max's signal. Not all of us are that talented."

"You can't whistle? Really?"

He stood. "Nope." He rolled the bike back and forth. "There we go. Looks good. Want to signal them for me, O Talented One?"

She couldn't see his expression, but she could sense the small smile in his voice. *Don't worry*, it said, *we'll all make it.* She wanted to believe him.

She whistled low, twice, and the group started up again. They were getting closer to the perimeter, cutting a path towards the edge of the city. It seemed to be getting darker, despite how black it was already.

The temperature continued to drop. She knew by the sound of the tires Max and Nate were up ahead, but she couldn't see them. Even her sister was little more than a shadow ahead of Aaron. The ground rose up in front of her and it was all she could do to keep focused on it. Shapes rushed by as long thin branches scraped against her arms and face, and a tangle of vegetation grabbed at her ankles and scratched at her calves. They were passing through the thin cropping of trees near the outskirts of the city. The wind shifted; she felt it even as they pushed their way through the brush, and then a low whistle sounded from somewhere up ahead. She pulled her brakes, and a brake squealed ahead of her. The cloud cover was too thick to see her own hands on her handlebar.

CHAPTER 18

"We're close," Max whispered from the darkness. "Our target is just ahead over this ridge. We only need a few minutes of moonlight and we're there."

"So, what, we just wait?" Nate asked through chattering teeth. If he was shivering … "How's Sam?"

"I'm okay." Her small voice carried back from a bike in front of them.

"I'm coming to you, Sam," Robyn whispered. Nate heard a bike hit the ground.

"Your hands are freezing," Sam said.

Nate grinned. Of course Robyn would be warming her sister. In fact, they should all be keeping warm.

"We need to stay ready," Max said, but his voice trembled.

"We need to get warm," Robyn said. "We're all going to get hypothermia standing here in the cold, not moving. Sam's frozen."

There was some rustling as another bike was set down. "Let me help," Trevor said. "The more of us huddled up around Sam, the more warmth we'll generate." Trevor joined them around Arron's handlebars.

Nate dropped his own bike. He'd never seen the night get so black. The cloud cover must be thick. He extended his arms out in from of him and walked towards them. Reaching out, his fingers finally found Robyn's icy arm, and he felt her jump at the unexpected touch. He pressed his body in close to hers, wrapping his arm around her shoulder, blocking Sam from the cold air.

"Let's get Sam warmed up while we wait for a little light," John said.

John put his arm around Nate, closing the tight circle around Sam. Trevor's arm was around Robyn's other shoulder, and her arms were wrapped around Nate's and Trevor's waists.

"Thanks," Sam whispered. "It's warmer.

As they surrounded her, Sam's shivering diminished, although Nate knew her skin would be frostbitten soon. Robyn shuffled a bit, probably trying to keep the blood flowing and her toes from freezing. She wound her fingers through the fabric of Nate's shirt.

"Isn't this cozy?" Nate asked after a moment. Someone chuckled.

"You know you've been looking for an excuse to hug Robyn since you met her, Coop," Trevor said.

"How about you, Trev?" Nate didn't bother denying it. "I'm sure you and your trainee here kept it totally platonic the whole time you were working together."

"Um, I'm right here, guys," she said.

"Keep it down," Max hissed from where he stood, still ready on his bike. Aaron silently steadied his bars.

They stood in huddled silence, their legs stiffening with both the cold and the lack of movement. Nate had been kidding when he said it was cozy, but it was also true. It *was* cozy. He could actually feel their breath as they inhaled and exhaled the same air within the circle. Of all the strange experiences he'd had over the last week, this was one of the few he didn't mind. He just wished his feet weren't so cold.

"Let's try again, slowly," Max finally said. "We can't afford to be caught out here in the light. The woods here are great cover at night but, in the morning, we'll be sitting ducks. Besides, the clouds have to clear eventually."

"You okay to go?" Robyn asked Sam.

"'Course," Sam said, and Nate let his arm drop from Robyn's shoulder. He instantly missed the warmth.

Time to go.

The others disappeared back into the darkness as they headed to their rides.

Nate groped for his bike, almost crawling. His fingers gripped the cold leather contour of his seat and he ran his hand along the chilled bar until it closed around the handlebars. He lifted the bike, almost losing his balance.

A quiet, low whistle sounded, and they started out, so slowly they were barely moving at all. There was a low thud and a sharp, muffled cry as someone obviously ran into a tree. Robyn's tires slid to a stop. It was a mistake. Nate cringed at the sound of grinding metal as Trevor plowed into the back of Robyn's bike, and at the faint click as his gears slipped again. Nate pulled his brakes to wait.

"Max," Robyn started.

"I know." His voice sounded strained.

Nate suspected the tree collision had been Max's.

"I guess we wait again until we can see more," Max said, "but let's hope the sky clears and the moon shows up before daylight. Do what you need to stay warm, but don't move far from your bike, and don't sleep." As if sleeping was even a mild possibility out here. "Be ready."

Nobody got off their bike this time. The wind was picking up. It wouldn't be long. Nate heard Trevor fiddling with his bike again. A moment later, moonlight filtered through the trees.

"How's the bike?" Nate asked Trevor.

"Good for now. Don't know how she'll do on the ride to the compound."

If we make it out of here, Nate added for him.

Max, who'd been waiting for Trevor to remount, signaled them forward, and they continued their way through the small woods. They were moving uphill now, zigzagging their way through the trees. Max picked up the pace, obviously trying to make up for the time they'd lost waiting for the light. The short break hadn't been helpful. Nate's muscles had started to seize and he'd lost momentum. He was already out of breath. He focused on ignoring the pain.

Robyn was panting up ahead. She had two perfectly functioning legs and could ride with both hands on the bars, so the fact she was exhausted made him feel a little better. He had to propel the bike with one working leg and, with his fixie, he couldn't even switch into a lower gear like the rest of them had.

"We're here," Max said, slowing to a stop just shy of the tree line.

So much for whistling.

Under the moonlit sky, the bridge over the river was clear.

"There's nobody there," Aaron said.

"Shh," Max said. He looked intently out into the clearing. Then, "We're too late. We'll have to go back."

"We're not too late," Aaron said. "Look. It's wide open."

At first, as far as Nate could tell, Aaron was right. Was

Max getting cold feet? Max gestured toward the distance and, as Nate scanned the length of the field ahead, two dimly lit shapes approached. Max knew what he was talking about. There wasn't time.

Nate felt for his gun. It wasn't there. He must have lost it somewhere along the way. Not that they could shoot their way out of this anyway.

Aaron's breathing was strange, though.

"Let's just wait," Robyn said, laying her hand on Aaron's arm. He shook her off.

Nate peered through the darkness at Aaron's face. Something was wrong.

"Aaron," Robyn tried again.

Without another word to anyone, Aaron pulled away from them, his tires spinning and throwing dirt and debris. Trevor reached out after him, yanking Sam from his bike just before Aaron emerged from the trees.

"Everyone get down," Max said.

It was too late for Aaron. Nobody could go after him without giving all of them away. Now all they could hope was he didn't get them all caught.

"I've got her," Trevor whispered as he and Sam lay flat, their bodies lost in the long grass. Nate hit the dirt beside Robyn, Max on his other side. John was the last one down.

Through the tall frosted blades, Nate saw Aaron nearing the bridge. He was almost certain he heard John's muffled sobs.

The two approaching shapes neared, becoming two patrolling Members on bikes. One held a torch in one hand as they rode. They were coasting at first but, as Aaron reached the bridge, there was a shout in the distance. He was halfway over when a single shot rang out in the dark followed rapidly by three more. Robyn flinched at each one.

Aaron's body dropped. The Members reached the bridge entrance and straddled their bikes, looking across at the still form. Another shot split the air. Nate knew the Members would dismount to investigate.

The one without the torch dropped his own bike and crossed the bridge. He knelt down beside Aaron. Nate heard a splash.

"Think there are more?" the man asked, walking Aaron's bike back across the bridge. He set it down and picked up his own again.

Nate pressed his face into the grass. The fallen branches dug into his skin, but he was careful not to move. The other man held out his torch, running it along the tree line. Nate barely breathed. Finally, the men rode back to their post by the bridge.

Aaron had sentenced them. How were they supposed to get out now? They were trapped. Trying to get up and back on their bikes and head out through the woods would be too noisy. There was no way they wouldn't be caught. And John had to be suffering, for another reason. How was the man's faith now?

Nate glanced back towards the bridge. Maybe if they went out of the woods one at a time, left their bikes and tried to make it back into the heart of the city on foot, they could individually pass for lost citizens. Maybe they could make it back home alive. Of course, Nate knew he'd be caught; he was pretty recognizable and they were looking for him. They couldn't really make it out on foot anyway, with the guards standing just feet away on high alert and with Sam's injured ankle. The smallest breaking branch would alert the guards.

As the cold seeped through his shirt, an idea occurred to him. It was crazy enough that it might work, maybe buy the small group enough time to get out. He leaned over to Max and quietly explained it. He knew Max would understand.

***

The grass rustled as Robyn shifted her body closer to his. "What's the plan?" she whispered, her voice so soft it was almost a breath.

"Max and I figured a way out of here."

"Oh yeah?"

"For everyone."

"How?"

"You'll see." He almost smiled.

"What do we do?"

"You need to stay really still until you guys get my signal. Then you just go. Get Sam up on John's bike. He's strong and steady. Then just ride for the bridge. Fast as you can."

"Signal?"

"Max is waiting for it."

"Okay." He knew she was worried, but this would work. It had to. And if it worked, this had to be goodbye.

"Don't freak out, okay?" Nate asked. He tugged at the fingertips of the glove from his good hand and pulled off the cold leather. He extended his hand and, very lightly, laid his palm on her cheek. He felt her flinch at the contact. "Sorry. I just want to see what your skin feels like without the stupid gloves. That okay?"

"Mm hmm," she said.

He slid his palm up and traced her brow line with his fingertips, then moved his thumb down her jaw and gently over her lips. He ran his thumb down to her chin, then back to rest on her cheek.

"Thanks for that," he whispered.

She seemed almost lost in his touch. It took a moment before she found her voice. "You're coming with us, right? Nate, we're not going without you."

"Listen." He moved his body closer now and felt her breath on his face, "I'm not a good person. Never will be. But you—"

"Nate ..."

"No, *listen*! Robyn, I'm worth nothing."

"You're not—"

"I am. You know the things I've done. I keep telling you, but you look at me like ... like I'm not that guy anymore." He forced the rest of the words out. "Like maybe my life could actually mean something to someone."

"Please don't go," she whispered, and hot tears ran down her cheeks onto his hand. "You mean something to me."

"And to think I didn't believe in miracles."

"Nate—"

"I meant it before when I said I wouldn't die for anyone."

"Good," she whispered.

He pulled his hand away from her face and slid his glove back on. "But I was wrong, Robyn."

CHAPTER 19

He didn't give her a chance to reply. Robyn reached out for him, but he was already gone. Gone before she could say anything to stop him, gone before she could say goodbye, gone before she could tell him …

"Tell the others to be ready," Max whispered to her.

She could barely think. Nate was planning to do something to get everyone out except himself. She knew it. There was no way he'd have told her what he did if he had expected to be back. And he hadn't taken his bike. He couldn't have. He was so quiet when he left he must have been on foot.

"Tell them," Max whispered again, not hearing her move.

She turned her head to her sister and Trevor. "Nate's gone to do something. Be ready."

"What's he doing?" Trevor's voice was thick with concern, echoing her horror.

"I don't know. Think it'll be something big. Tell John."

"He's coming back, right?" Sam asked.

"Shhh." If Robyn told her the truth, that she was pretty sure Nate had no intention of making it out alive, Sam would refuse to go.

Trevor whispered to John, warning him to be ready.

The smell of smoke began to fill the air. About a mile down the road, flames licked the edges of the wooded area. Nate must have set it on fire. The guards noticed it at the same time she did, and they took off towards the fire on their bikes. A fire like that could get out of control. Others, from farther down the way, ripped past towards it. The bridge was empty.

"Now!" Max's whisper broke the silence.

Robyn grabbed Sam and lifted her onto the front of John's bike.

"You're going to have to hold tight," John said.

Then Max was on his feet, grabbing his bike and pedaling across to wait at the bridge. John and Trevor were up next and followed.

Robyn tore her eyes away and reached for her bike. As she pulled it up, its weight felt wrong. Her feet touched the small, jagged pedals, designed for those shoes, and she knew she'd grabbed Nate's fixie instead. *Good enough.*

She didn't bother looking for her own bike. As she reached the others, John was waiting.

"You have to keep going with Sam," she told them, realizing the real reason she'd been glad she took Nate's bike instead of her own. "Please. I can't go without him."

"I'm not going without him either," Trevor said. He looked at John. "I know you feel like you need to stay here in the city, but …"

"I'll wait with Sam for you at the edge of the forest after No Man's Land," John said. "If you're not back by daybreak, I'll get Sam to the garrison without you. I've been waiting to hear from God that I've done all I can and that it's time to go. This must be it."

She expected Sam to argue or fight them, but everything was happening too quickly, and Sam would want Nate with them. Sam's silence was the permission Robyn needed.

John turned to Max. "Get home to your wife."

Max nodded without hesitation. Robyn didn't blame him. He didn't owe Nate anything. He'd done as much as he could for them and he had other promises to keep. He disappeared back into the woods.

"Take care of each other," Robyn whispered to Sam. Samantha nodded before she John disappeared over the bridge.

Robyn almost expected the patrol to reappear. But she couldn't even see them anymore, the cover of smoke was so thick. And it was getting hard to breathe.

"You sure you want to do this?" Trevor asked. "Your sister's on the other side of the river. For all we know, Nate might already be dead. Probably is. From the fire or the patrol."

"I have to know." It was all she could say.

"It was his choice to make." Trevor stared in the direction of the bridge. She followed his gaze. "He would have wanted you safe on the other side and heading off into the sunset with your family, not riding blindly into the exact thing he was trying to save you from."

"And you?"

"Coop would have expected me to come for him. No matter what."

She almost laughed. Of course Trevor saw himself as Nate's guardian angel. Maybe he was, in his own way. "He thinks you're the only one who's ever cared about him."

"He's wrong."

She wasn't sure if Trevor was talking about God now or about her. She didn't have time to think about it anyway. It was getting impossible to see.

She tore her gaze from the bridge. "I'm coming with you to get Nate. You might as well save yourself the argument. So what do we do now?"

"I guess we try to circle around, see if we can find Nate."

"And if we do?"

"We'll figure it out when we get there." He glanced into the darkened woods. The fire was spreading quickly, jumping treetop to treetop.

They headed towards the trees, but when they reached the edge where the overgrown field blended into the tangled shrubs and bush, the smoke was so thick they couldn't see anything at all. Riding through the trees wasn't going to happen.

"Looks like we're taking the main road," she said.

"Looks that way. Still not praying?" When she didn't answer, he added, "Now might be a good time to start." He stood on his bike now, pedaling slowly towards where the Members would be trying to stop the fire. Even if he were kidding, she had a pretty strong feeling he was talking silently to his God even now. John, too.

As they neared the source of the fire, the shouts were louder and water hissed as the Members futilely worked to put out the flames.

Please was all she could muster. *Please let Nate be alive. Please let us get out of here.*

A crowd of Members was up ahead. They had a multi-bucket pulley system rigged up, one they'd made to collect water. They were using it to bring water up from the river, a line of Members running it to the forest.

"Are we just riding right up to them?" she whispered.

"When people are distracted, they miss the facts right in

front of their eyes." Trevor drew in a slow breath, then let it out. "Be confident."

Confident. Easier said than done.

As they approached, she could see someone lying on the ground. One of the Members stood with his boot hard on the figure's back. As they drew closer, she could make out dark cargo pants and that familiar tousled hair. *Nate*. He wasn't moving.

"Is he …" she whispered to Trevor, barely able to choke out the words. She had to know though. How could she bear not knowing?

"Look." He nodded towards Nate.

The guard had Nate's arms twisted around his back. It was why he was standing on him like that: he was preventing him from escaping. Tears stung Robyn's eyes. Nate was alive.

"Here goes nothing," Trevor said under his breath. He coasted forward.

She quickly wiped her cheeks with the side of her hand and followed him, willing herself to be calm.

Confident.

"Hey," Trevor called.

She started at the tone and volume of his voice. It was like he wanted the whole world to see him there.

"Hey," the guy standing atop Nate answered. "You relief?"

"Kind of," Trevor said. "We're supposed to take that piece of garbage in. Partner's looking out for anyone who might be working with him or waiting somewhere to try to rescue him."

"Think he's the guy Marshall's looking for?"

"That's what I'm supposed to find out."

"How you gonna take him in on that?" he asked, eying Trevor's bike. "Guy's a cripple. Can barely walk."

"That's what I meant by 'kind of,'" Trevor said. He swung

his leg off the bike. "Walking him in. Supposed to bring a ride to anyone who could use a shift break."

"Sounds good." Any suspicion the guy might have felt seemed to vanish at the offer of Trevor's superior bike.

Robyn swallowed. Trevor'd had it since he was a kid. It was all that was left of his old life … and he was just handing it over like it meant nothing.

The patrol eased his foot off Nate, and Trevor hauled him up. She could tell Nate was suppressing a grin; his eyes were laughing. Nate shifted his gaze to hers and the merriment drained from his expression when he saw her standing there. He frowned, averting his eyes.

"Come on," Trevor said.

She rolled her bike around and followed him. For someone who'd burnt down a forest and gotten himself caught trying to protect her, he didn't seem very happy to see her.

Forcing themselves to go slowly, they passed the area where the greatest congestion of Members was.

"They'll never be able to stop that thing," Trevor said as they approached the bridge.

"I know. But the forest's far enough away from the city I figured it should be okay. Plus my bad leg hurts. Means rain," Nate said.

"You know that's just an urban legend," Robyn said.

Nate didn't reply. He'd told her before he was ready to die for her. Now he wouldn't even look at her.

"What are we gonna do now?" Nate asked. "We don't have enough bikes. And I left mine in the trees. So—"

"Robyn brought your fixie," Trevor said, gesturing to the bike Robyn was walking behind them. "She can take Aaron's. The Members just left it here when the fire started.

"You and I can double up," she said to Trevor, "or …"

"I'm not going," Trevor said, holding up his hand as they both started to protest. "John's going home to his family. It's about time he did. But someone needs to stay here and take his place."

Nate shook his head. "And it's gotta be you."

"Yeah."

"Doesn't hurt that Stacie's staying too, hey?"

He shrugged. "I don't know. Guess so."

Robyn wasn't surprised. In fact, she was relieved. Trevor may not have figured out his own feelings yet but, one day, he would have woken up and realized he should never have left that girl behind. "So how are you getting back?"

"I'll walk it. It's a long way, but I'm strong. Nobody will recognize me—I'm just some guy out for a stroll."

She expected Nate to argue or to try and convince him, but Nate extended his hand. Trevor reached out to shake it and then pulled Nate into a hug. When he let him go, Trevor turned to face her. "You know you still gotta make it to the garrison without me. Think you can handle it?"

"Guess I'm going to find out." She smiled weakly at him, and then it was her turn to be wrapped in his strong arms.

"Don't worry about Nate," he whispered into her ear. "He thought he was never going to see you again. He's scared."

Nate? Scared?

They stopped once more at the bridge. Trevor righted Aaron's bike. She took it from him and handed the fixie to Nate.

"See you around." Trevor's voice was suddenly hoarse.

Nate didn't look back as he clicked into his pedals and started over the bridge, but he raised his hand in a silent wave.

"Thanks for everything," Robyn whispered. With a final

look, she turned and followed Nate across the river.

She caught up easily. He didn't look at her. "Where are the others?"

"Max went back. John and Sam are waiting for us just outside of No Man's Land."

No Man's Land. The term they'd given to the large expanse of open field after the river and before the provincial park's campground, with its sparse trees and what used to be a labyrinth of bicycle trails. She knew, because when she'd come to visit her aunt here, they had promised her she'd get to ride the trails. So much for that idea. Less than a day after she'd arrived, the blackout hit. A week after that, her aunt and uncle died trying to get out of town. And then her parents had been killed by the Grims.

From the provincial park, it was several miles to the farmers' garrisons. The tree line was ahead but there was no sign of her sister or John. Had they gone on ahead without her?

I hope so. The idea of her sister and John safe within the garrison was comforting.

"There they are." John's bike leaned against a tree. He was sitting on the ground beside the bike, with Sam cradled on his lap. They both rose when they saw Nate and Robyn approaching, although Sam leaned against John.

"I knew you'd bring him!" Sam called out. She looked past Nate to Robyn. "Where's Trevor?"

"Trev decided to stay," Nate answered.

"Why?"

"He said someone needs to fill this guy's shoes." Nate gestured to where John stood leaning against the tall, thin oak tree on the edge of the park.

"Feels right. He'll do good," John said.

"Are we setting up camp for the night?" Nate asked.

Camp. The word implied tents and sleeping bags, roasted marshmallows, and ghost stories. That obviously wasn't what he meant.

"Yeah," John said. "It's too cold and dark to make it through the provincial park tonight. We don't want to attract the attention of predators either. We'll sleep for a few hours until sunrise, then get on our way. It's still a pretty long stretch before the farmers' garrison. With any luck, nobody from River Ridge will even know we made it out."

Robyn shivered. "We're going to need some heat."

"Shouldn't be a problem. Sam and I already found some old campsites, complete with fire pits and fairly level ground. Fire should keep away the wildlife visitors, and we'll be well enough hidden by the trees to prevent anyone from the city seeing us."

With Sam back on his handlebars, John led Nate and Robyn down the dark, overgrown path. The leaves crunched under their tires. Although it had been over two years since most people had used the paths, the grass alongside them had not grown completely in; enough Members still rode along them when they were out hunting. As she followed the natural bend of the muddy trail, Robyn couldn't help but imagine how it would have felt flying along here at full speed, back when riding was pleasure. If the paths were anything like those back home, summers would have found the park teeming with cyclists.

As they passed through a narrow opening between two large spruce trees, she imagined the spot where the bark would be worn from the handlebars of riders clipping it as they misjudged their distances. She would have loved to tear down this path some summer afternoon, the sun bright through the sparse treetops and mud flying up from her tires.

People deserved to feel that again.

"It's right up here," John called back to them.

The path widened as it descended into a small vale. They entered a clearing with a black metallic fire pit at its center. Beside it lay a long log that must have, at one time, served as a makeshift bench. The clearing would have been big enough for a large camper or a couple of tents and a vehicle.

Robyn laid her bike on the grass and gently lifted her sister from John's. He laid his bike down beside hers.

"Should I start collecting firewood?" Robyn asked.

"No. I'll go," John said. "You stay and warm the little one up."

"I'll get started on the fire," Nate said. "Hurry, John"

Robyn sat down and pulled Sam onto her lap. Her sister tucked in close, and Robyn wrapped her in her arms the best she could. Nate, hunched over the fire pit, worked with his lighter and the kindling he'd collected from the campsite while John was gathering more wood to maintain it. A small flame smoldered within the bowl at first, and then it burst into light as the brushwood caught flame.

"Come in closer," he said. "Sam must be freezing."

"I am." Sam's voice was soft. She was shivering. Robyn picked her up and carried her in front of the log bench. Robyn sat down close to the fire, with Sam snuggled in on her lap.

Soon footsteps crunched through the leaves in the brush. They looked up to see John with his hands full of branches. "I didn't get as much as I'd hoped. I really didn't want to spend too much time digging around in the dirt. You know there's gotta be snakes in there." As he finished speaking, an animal howled in the distance.

Sam didn't say anything but she moved even closer in to Robyn. Robyn wrapped her arms more tightly around her sister.

"Not that long till morning, though, so this should last us," John said.

Nate limped over to John and took the wood from him. "I'll make sure it does." He crossed back to the fire and added a few branches. After stacking the small pile of wood that remained, he sat down beside Robyn.

John came and sat on the ground on the other side of the fire. "We should be okay." He was speaking mostly to himself, it seemed, as he peered out into the night. Light was already on the horizon. There were only a few hours, at most, until daybreak.

Robyn felt Sam's body relax as she stared into the flickering flame. Soon, her sister's breathing became slow and regular. John, too, had slumped over and lay asleep on his side. For such a big man, he seemed child-like in sleep.

Nate hadn't drifted off yet. She heard him playing with a stick beside her. She knew it was his intention to stay awake and keep the fire stoked.

Her eyes felt heavy. She leaned her head back on the log behind her.

"You awake?" Nate asked after a moment.

"Uh huh," she replied.

"I didn't do it."

"What?"

"I didn't kill your folks. I wasn't there. I'd remember it."

"Oh."

"I didn't tell you before, but I meant to."

"Oh." She didn't really know what to say. Maybe she'd known it all along, or maybe it was too painful to even think about. Maybe it was a lifetime ago.

"Uh huh."

They lapsed into silence again.

Finally, she asked, "Why were you so mad at me? When I came back for you?"

"Because I wanted you safe. I didn't want you to risk yourself for me."

"It wasn't your call. There was no way I could just let you do that. I couldn't go without you, Nate."

He didn't respond right away, and she let the words hang in the air. Staring into the flames, the comfortable haze of sleep was overcoming her senses.

"Robyn?" he asked, rousing her slightly.

"Uh huh?"

"Why couldn't you go without me?"

"You know why."

CHAPTER 20

"Wake up!" Nate's frantic voice called out to Robyn through the darkness.

She opened her eyes to the early light of dawn. Sam stirred beside her while John got to his feet.

"They're coming. I hear them," Nate said. He was right. Men's voices shouted to one another. They weren't far off.

"Farmers?" she asked.

"No way. Not this close to the city," John said. "We need to move."

She peered out into the trees. Flashes of red in the distance worked their way through the paths and over the grass.

"Now." John looked at Nate. "You okay to ride?"

"'Course," Nate replied. "But Sam can't. There's no way she'd be able to stay on handlebars riding at full speed over the trails here."

"You have to hide." Robyn picked up Sam.

"No! You can't leave me!" She kicked her legs. "You can't!"

Robyn stopped and met her sister's eyes. "Sam. I love you. You are my whole world. But if they find you, if they hurt you, I couldn't go on living. Do you understand that?"

"But I can't—"

"You *can*. We'll come back for you. I promise." She said it with such conviction she almost believed it.

"You can't promise that." Nate's voice startled her. "What if they catch up with us? What will happen to Sam out here?"

"Nate!"

"No." John circled around the smoldering pit towards her. "Nate's right. You need to get down under the brush with your little sister and hide. Keep her quiet and safe. Nate and I will lead them away." John must have known Robyn was never going to agree, because he grabbed her bike with both hands, hoisted it up, and flung it, hard, into the brush. John picked up his own bike. "We'll give them a clear target. Something to chase. Something to draw them away from Sam." She opened her mouth to protest, but it was too late. Riders were coming and she had no time to retrieve the bike.

"Hide." Nate touched her arm. "We'll get to the garrison and get help. Just wait for us. Please."

"Nate—"

His hand slid from her arm to wrap around her waist. He yanked her tight against his chest, and his lips met hers with all the urgency and grief and passion of another goodbye.

And then he was gone. Robyn grabbed Sam and carried her as far away from the small clearing as she could, into thick, deep grass. She lay down flat with Sam, close to a large tree trunk. They would be almost invisible here.

Robyn lifted her head. John flew down the trail, with Nate's front tire almost touching John's back one. In the distance, just over a crest, she saw a rider pull into one of the tracks running parallel to theirs. John saw him, too, and sharply veered off onto another path. This path was thinner, barely visible; he must have known these trails from before, to have found it so quickly. Nate followed, but he wasn't as quick at the turns and his bike wavered. He slowed—not by much—but enough so the rider was almost upon him. *Please, Nate, hurry.*

She knew the woods were filling up with Members. She could only hope they could somehow outride them enough to get away.

***

Nate followed John down the narrow path. It would only be a matter of time until they were caught. There was no way he could outrun them and he wasn't sure John was a match for Marshall's men either. They knew these woods.

He pushed forward, branches hitting him across the face as he moved. John was barely visible through the thick brush ahead.

Shouts echoed from far off to his right.

"Let's split up. Give them two rabbits!" Nate shouted to John.

"You got it."

"Go." He veered off.

"I'll come find you." John disappeared down the other path.

Nate knew if he or John were caught, they'd try to get information about Robyn from him. He'd die first.

More shouts echoed through the woods. Where were they coming from? Had they caught John yet?

He could make out the remnants of another path ahead and another one after that. These woods were filled with them: a winding maze of interconnected deer trails. He turned down the first. His chances of finding a way out were slim. But maybe he'd …

He pulled his brakes hard as a Member appeared over the

crest in front of him and rode full tilt towards him. He tried to turn his bike but there was no room. Branches hemmed him in and the overgrown path made maneuvering next to impossible. Even as he unclipped his cleats and yanked his bike, its weight pushed on his good leg. He lost his balance and toppled into the bush, sharp branches scraping against his arms and digging into his calves. The weight of the bike pinned him down. He wished he still had his gun. At the very least, he could have made sure they didn't take him alive.

The Member approached.

A red bandana.

A Grim.

"Ha. If it isn't the cripple," he said, grinning down at Nate.

"Hey, Berg," Nate said, recognizing Marshall's lieutenant. "Long time no see."

"Glad for a chance to catch up." Berg pulled out a black zip tie from his hoodie. Leaning over the bike, he grabbed Nate's hands, ignoring his struggle, and twisted them behind his back. He tied Nate's wrists together in a fluid motion.

Berg had been Marshall's muscle long before the blackout. He knew what he was doing. With one thick hand, he heaved Nate's bike out of the way, then hauled Nate up by his shirt. He pushed him out in front of him. "Walk."

When Nate didn't move, he shoved him. Nate let his knees buckle. Berg would take him to Marshall, and there was no way they were planning on a quick death. They'd use him to find Robyn and the others.

Nate didn't intend to make it easier for them.

"Get up." Berg's voice was quiet, controlled.

Nate didn't move. He heard the rustle of leaves and grass and then the toe of Berg's boot slammed into his ribs.

A scream tore itself from his throat in spite of his resolve, and he curled himself into a ball. Berg kicked him again, connecting this time with Nate's bad leg. As he twisted away from the boots, a sharp pain radiated through his lower back. Berg just missed his spine.

"I said get up," Berg told him. He kicked him again, and then again and again.

Nate fought against the black threatening to swallow him. He struggled to breathe through the pain and, when Berg moved his leg back again, Nate held up a hand.

"Okay," Nate said.

He'd never seen himself as weak before, not even after the fire, but it seemed pointless to have Berg beat him half to death here, not when he knew Berg wouldn't finish the job. Eventually, Nate would have to do what the guy wanted. He might as well save his energy for Marshall. Besides, there was no way for Berg to let Marshall know they'd caught him, and Marshall wouldn't call off the hunt until he knew Nate had been captured. He'd just have to make sure Marshall killed him before they could use him to get to Robyn and the others. He'd have to do something, say something, make Marshall lose it. And to do that, he'd have to stay conscious.

"Help me up," Nate said, after he caught his breath.

Berg laughed, pulling Nate to his feet. "Dead weight, as usual." He shoved him, and Nate started walking.

It hurt to breathe. Nate was pretty sure Berg had fractured something, a rib, maybe. He missed the days of hospitals. Everyone used to complain about a broken healthcare system, but it had been a whole lot better than what they had now. He could definitely use a doctor. Or at least some good painkillers.

He allowed Berg to direct him down the path. He focused on

keeping his pace steady. It was a strange thing to be purposefully hurrying towards his own death. But it was inevitable.

Death is what happens …

Up ahead, the trees broke into a clearing. Voices fell silent as he stepped from the tree line. Marshall stood with a small group. He grinned: a too-wide, hard smile.

Berg's hands were hard on Nate's back.

"The man of the hour," Marshall said as Berg's shove sent Nate sprawling on his stomach at Marshall's feet. Before he could get up, Marshall's tread pressed hard against the side of Nate's face, pushing his cheek into the grass.

Nate struggled, ignoring the pain. Marshall wanted an excuse to escalate things, and Nate was happy to give it to him. If he were dead, it would be over. For everyone.

"Cooper, my boy," Marshall said, increasing the pressure, "we're going to have fun this afternoon. Show you what it means to betray your family. Remind the others what we do to traitors. Make an—" Marshall looked up at a shout from across the park. "Ah. Things are getting interesting."

Nate's heart sunk as Marshall removed his boot and Berg hauled him to his feet. Across the field, men walked John towards him, at gunpoint.

***

They'd seen her bike lying in the bush. Robyn could hear three of them combing the bushes somewhere behind her. They'd be on her any minute now.

She looked at her sister, trembling beside her. They wouldn't care that Sam was a kid, an innocent. They'd only care that she was with them. But right now, they didn't know Sam existed. One bike, one rider.

She could hear the footsteps, closer still. Robyn squeezed her sister's hand. "Stay hidden until the woods are quiet." She kept her voice a whisper. "I'm going to lead them away. If I haven't come back by the time the sun starts to get low, you're going to have to try to make it back to the city. It's gonna hurt, but you'll have to do it. Just follow the path out of the woods, back the way we came. You can see the city from the edge of the forest."

Her sister whimpered and shook her head.

"I'm planning to come back, Sam. This is just in case. If they know you're with us, they'll hurt you. But right now, they don't really know you exist. If you can make it back to the city, pretend you're just some kid whose parents died on the road somewhere. They might help. They're not all monsters." She didn't know if it were true or not, but she hoped so. What choice did she have? The Members were almost on them now. Only a few feet away now.

"Love you," she whispered, then stood. She bolted past them towards where John had thrown her bike. Shouts rose from behind her as they yanked their bikes to reverse their direction, but she was fast. She grabbed her bike and threw her leg over, pedaling hard. Had all three given chase?

She was coming to a steep incline. The track slanted upwards and then sharply curved to the left. She was already riding at full speed. She leaned her body forward, hoping the momentum would carry her over the crest. Her tire spun, throwing dirt in a stream behind her as she muscled her way up the hill. She made it around the turn, feeling the wheels slide in the loose soil as they fought for traction.

Following the lines of the overgrown path, Robyn saw it was beginning a downward slope. She would have coasted this section, appreciating the brief respite after the hard climb, if she'd been out here on vacation.

Instead, she used the drop to gain speed, pedaling hard

to overtake the quick roll of her wheels. The riders behind her were gaining speed, too, and the tread of a tire behind her grazed her rear wheel. Reaching above her head, she grabbed a thin, overhanging branch and let it go. It flung back, catching the rider off guard, and she heard him hit his brake, slide out and crash through the brush. Someone shouted behind her as another person, likely swerving to avoid the fallen Member, collided with a tree. She glanced over her shoulder. Two bikes were strewn out behind her and a rider lay motionless against a tree, but two more Members had managed to swerve around the accident and had pulled back onto the trail behind her.

She looked ahead just in time to see the trail dip forward. She rode through a small creek, the water soaking her sneakers and the mud caking her tires, slowing her down. A splash behind her meant another rider was down. Pedaling hard through ice-cold water, she saw where the path continued up head. She was almost there. She scanned the brush. There had to be another path. A small thinning of the trees not far away was her best shot; an animal trail, too narrow to have ever been used for cyclists. She jerked her bike around and pulled onto it. She knew the distance between her and the closest pursuer was widening.

She had no idea what direction she was headed in now. She didn't even know where she wanted to be. Her only plan was to lose them, to somehow get clear. If she couldn't, maybe she could at least lead them on a long enough chase to give John, Nate, and her sister time to get away.

Members rode through the bush towards her, aiming to cut her off. She turned into the woods on the other side of the trail, crashing through the foliage. She didn't see the sharp rock jutting out of the ground up ahead; the edge of her tire skimmed it, almost sending her into a slide. She caught herself, touching her foot down, then regained her balance, but the mistake had cost her. They were closing in again from all sides.

Robyn pushed towards a small clearing where the trees seemed to open into an overgrown field. She flew down the path and into the clearing. A small plastic play structure, with its faded paint and the remnants of a worn, green, wooden bench, stood just past a wide service road. Two figures knelt in the fine sand beneath the climbing rods of what used to be the provincial park's playground. She gasped, her feet motionless for a moment, and then her bike jerked to a stop as she hit a rut. As she flew over her handlebars, she realized she was probably going to die today.

CHAPTER 21

Robyn came to, face down in the white sand, her hands tied behind her back. The thin zip tie bit into the skin of her wrists and the sand was rough against her cheek. Someone nudged her with what felt like a boot.

"Wakey, wakey," a voice said. She opened her eyes. "Ah, there we go."

Rough hands hauled her to her knees beside Nate. His nose was bleeding. Bruises had already begun to form along his cheek. His right eye was swollen shut. On his other side was John, his face pale, a deep gash along his temple. John's eyes were closed. Was he still alive?

"Robyn?" Sam knelt in the sand beside her, little wrists bound together.

No. Please, no.

Robyn struggled against the ropes. It was no use. There was a blinding flash of pain as one of her captors shot out with his fist. She hit the sand, tasting blood.

"No!" Sam's shrill voice split the air.

"Don't ..." Nate said, at the same time. Before he could

finish, there was the sound of bone on flesh and he hit the ground beside her.

The world spun and she squeezed her eyes shut, trying to regain her bearings. She opened her eyes as someone yanked Nate up, then pulled her to her knees again. She focused on staying steady, trying to keep herself from falling over. They were surrounded by the twelve or thirteen Members who'd chased them through the park. Sam sobbed beside her.

"It's okay, Sam. Just close your eyes." She wished she could wrap her arms around her little sister. She should have known Sam wouldn't have stayed there without her. "Keep them closed. It's okay. Promise."

A large man stood over them, his fist balled up at his side. A satisfied smile played on his lips.

Sam whimpered, squeezing her eyes closed. *Please just let my sister go,* Robyn wanted to beg. *She's just a kid.* Begging would only encourage them. Even as she focused on willing her sister to stay silent, to not draw attention to herself, Robyn shook, drowning in fear and pain.

The man stepped towards her again.

"Come on, Berg," Nate said, his voice muffled by his swollen jaw. "She's just scared. She's got nothing to with this."

Nothing to do with this?

"Guilt by association," another man's controlled voice stated from behind her. "Will we have any more issues?"

Robyn stared at Berg's knuckles, smeared with Nate's blood. She shook her head.

"Good." The man from behind her stepped out past Nate and turned to look at them. His face was neutral, his hands calmly clasped in front of him. "So, you're the lot who killed my son."

"I told you it was me, Marshall," Nate said. Berg's thick fist instantly connected with Nate's chin, knocking him down into the sand.

Robyn winced, glancing away in time to see Sam's eyes fly open, gaze locked on Robyn's face. Was Sam remembering that day under the suburban?

"Promise." Robyn mouthed the words, and Sam pinched her eyes closed again.

"Guilt by association," Marshall said again. When Marshall nodded, Berg pulled Nate back to his knees.

"How'd you find us?" Nate asked, his voice unsteady. He flinched as the first man moved towards him again.

Marshall raised a hand, stopping Berg. "One of my men told me that the guy I'd sent to retrieve you was bringing you in. Obviously, I hadn't sent anyone, so we came looking for you. We found an abandoned bike in the trees this morning, just across from the roadway blockade."

They hadn't found Trevor. Nate had to be relieved. She wished she could reach out and squeeze his hand.

"And now, here you are," Marshall said. "The question is, what should I do with you?"

"Let us go?" Nate was answered by another blow across his face.

Sam's eyes stayed shut this time but she couldn't quiet the sobs shaking her body.

"What I'm trying to decide is whether to execute you now or show you how upsetting I find it when my own men cross me." Marshall's voice rose. "And then execute you afterwards."

Without warning, Berg leaned over and struck Nate across the face again. As he fell, Berg booted him in the ribs, driving his body into the sand. Berg circled, then his foot connected with Nate's back. Nate writhed in pain as he was hauled back up to his knees. Head drooping, he spit blood in Berg's direction. Berg ambled over to the green wooden bench near the edge of the playground. He leaned his foot on the seat and pried off one of the long wooden slats from the backing, breaking it halfway down.

"Please don't," Robyn whispered as Berg stepped towards Nate, the plywood resting on his shoulder.

John's eyelids fluttered and he groaned as he roused to consciousness.

Nate raised his gaze to her. He shook his head.

Berg was going to kill him, and Nate wanted her to—what? Just be quiet about it? Let it happen?

"Please, please stop. Please." She barely recognized her own voice, thick with desperation. "It was all my fault. My fault."

Berg stopped.

The words poured out of her like a confession. Like a last confession. "I took the bike. I let that guy die. I got Jared killed. It was me. Please. It was my fault."

Marshall jerked his head towards her, and Berg grabbed the back of her neck with his free hand, hauling her backwards. Screaming, she struggled against his grasp. Her sister's wail rose up, and John called her name. The next thing she knew she was facedown, a strong, heavy hand keeping her there. Closing her lips, she fought for breath, trying to turn her face away from the suffocating press of sand so she wouldn't black out. Finally, he yanked her back up and threw her down on her back.

She inhaled deep, gulping in oxygen.

"Interesting," Marshall said. "Get her up."

Berg reached over and yanked Robyn to her feet.

Marshall took a step. He stared into Robyn's face,

expressionless. His hand flicked to his waistband, and cold steel pressed hard against her temple.

Sam and John were begging for her life. Their words flowed together in an endless stream, but all she could hear was Nate.

"Stop." Nate's voice cracked. He struggled to stand, arms still bound behind his back. "Please, don't … don't do this …"

She pictured Marshall pulling the trigger. Would she feel it? Or would she just wake up … where? She thought about the forgiveness John had been talking about. She didn't want to die before—

"Please, Marshall!" Nate said.

She listened to the click as he cocked the hammer and all she could think was, *I'm not ready. Please, not yet.*

"I'm so sorry, Robyn." Tears streamed down Nate's cheeks. "Please, Marshall. I'll do anything. Please …"

She'd never seen him cry. Even with the beating he'd endured. Now he bawled, begging for her life.

They were out of time.

A crack sounded and Sam screamed. For a second, Robyn thought he'd fired. Another one followed, closer this time, and she looked up to find the source. Two men on horses rode at a gallop from the service road towards them, their rifles pointed high in the air. As they neared, they shifted the barrels to aim at the Members. Marshall lowered his gun for a second, then brought it up and pointed it at the approaching men.

"Drop your weapon," one of the men on horseback yelled.

Nobody moved.

"I'm not afraid of you!" Marshall shouted. He lowered his arm to press the muzzle against Nate's cheek.

"Bad idea." The voice came from behind her. There, standing just outside the tree line, were about a dozen armed farmers, their weapons drawn and aimed. "You shoot that man there, and you and your men don't make it out of here alive. Now, be smart. Drop it."

Marshall's hand began to shake.

She knew Marshall must be considering. He had Nate. He could take his revenge if he wanted it. But he'd lose everything in the city he'd been working towards—and his chance for revenge on the rest of them. If Marshall died now, he'd never get it. She was counting on him realizing that. They all were.

With a guttural cry, Marshall moved the gun off Nate's cheek, then tossed it out beside him.

"Go home," the first rider said.

The men on horseback waited, watching the flurry of motion as the Members got back onto their bikes and disappeared down the trails. A few of the armed farmers swung around to follow them out. The sound of tires and hoofs on dirt faded. Robyn knew Marshall wasn't done, that he'd regroup and come looking for them, but they'd be gone by the time he made it back.

"You folks okay?" Their rescuer climbed down off his horse and cut the zip tie that bound her hands behind her back while another farmer freed Sam. It took only moments. Robyn crawled over to her sister and threw her arms around her.

"We're all right now," Robyn said into her sister's hair. "We're all right."

She looked over Samantha's shoulder at Nate. The man finished untying him and Nate took an unsteady step toward her. John, also freed, clasped his shoulder, and he turned and allowed John to embrace him.

"You're lucky you all made so much noise," the man said, signaling the rest of his riders forward now that the Grims were out of gunshot range. "A couple of the boys were out hunting when they heard the commotion. Figured it might be refugees from the city in some trouble, so they sent word. Came as quick as we could.

"They were looking for me," Nate said. He looked terrible. His eye was even more swollen and his face was a mess of blood and bruises.

"Looks like they found you." The man whistled, and they followed his gaze back down the service road. Two horses came up the road, pulling a large wagon. "Taxi's here."

"Amen," John said, his familiar smile somehow finding its way back onto his lips. He looked at the men as the cart pulled up and extended his large hand. "John Ashwood."

"Weston Peters," the man said, then cocked his head. "You have a wife—Ellie—and a little one living with us?"

"I do."

"They'll be happy to see you. Been praying for you."

"He's been listening." John allowed the smaller man to help him into the wagon.

"Your turn," Weston said, reaching out for Sam.

"You're coming, right, Robyn?" Sam asked.

"Promise." She waited as her sister was lifted into the wagon. Sam crawled across the wagon bed to where John sat against the wall; she rested her head against his arm. Nate limped to the edge of the wagon. Instead of offering to help him up, Weston extended his arm to him, allowing Nate to use it to climb into the box.

Nate leaned against the wall opposite John. Robyn pulled herself into the wagon and sat down beside him. Sam grinned.

As Weston and his partner rigged their bikes to the back, he said, "Be only a short while till we're at the garrison. You're safe now."

Safe.

Minutes before, she was sure she was dead. Now, just like that, she was *safe*. She looked across the wagon at John's relaxed confidence.

Nate nudged her. "Maybe John's not completely crazy," he whispered.

Finished with the bikes, Weston swung himself back on his horse and whistled to his men. The wagon lurched to an uneven start and then began down the open road towards what would be their new home. As they turned onto the empty highway, Robyn looked out at the tall oak trees—their orange and yellow leaves, bright in the daylight, seemed to wave as they passed. Even with the late November chill, the morning sun was warm on her skin.

She moved closer to Nate, allowing their shoulders to touch. He reached for her hand, intertwining his fingers with hers.

Note to the Reader

Thanks for reading *Ride to Daylight*.

If you enjoyed it, please tell a friend. Tell ten! And, if you have a few minutes, please consider stopping by your favorite online bookseller or review site and leaving a review. Nothing helps a book—or an author—like a good recommendation from a fan.

Want to connect with the author? Find her on Instagram and Twitter, or check out her website at www.alyssathiessen.ca.

Other Books by Alyssa Thiessen

AMBER RAIN

Sixteen-year-old Ellie Lauder doesn't belong. Although she's grown up in the underground shelter with the descendants of those who survived the amber rain, their rejection drives her to a dangerous course of action. She flees outside to a vast wilderness that, according to what she's been taught, shouldn't even exist. This frightening new world seems to hold the key to her hidden past—if she can survive long enough to find it.

DRAGONFLY

Joshua Miller is great at being invisible, despite the insect-like wings protruding from his back and his knack for high-rise robberies. He's alone—the villain in his own story—and he likes it that way. But then Joshua unexpectedly meets Lexi on a job, and his simple, uncomplicated existence shifts. Where he sees only darkness, she shows him light. When a split-second decision alters his life forever, Joshua embarks on a quest to discover who he is. Is he really destined to be the bad guy, or can this Dragonfly find a way back to the hero within?

INFUSION

Rachel is ordinary. Normal. Utterly unremarkable... until her best friend shoots her on her 16th birthday and a stranger brings her from death's doorstep with an infusion of his own DNA. Then everything gets weird. She heals impossibly fast. She senses the thoughts of others. She sees places and horrifying creatures that couldn't possibly exist, and her hot new friend Tyler is convinced she's destined to save the world from an invasion. But how's she supposed to stop inter-dimensional invaders when she can barely deal with high school?

Ready or not, here they come.

SHORT STORIES BY ALYSSA THIESSEN

EYES ON THE LAKE

(in CANADIAN CREATURES, an anthology published Schreyer Ink

On his 21st birthday, David and Annalise set out on British Columbia's Okanagan lake, searching for the truth in a childhood memory. Did David really see a Mermaid all those years ago?

Sometimes, truth is more terrifying than fiction.

GLASS

(in BLANK SPACES MAGAZINE, Volume 3, Issue 4, a Canadian Literary Arts magazine)

A young woman in a crowded club encounters a shadow from her past. At first, as she makes her way through the room towards him, Emma Wilson sees a second chance.

Then, she sees who she really is and what matters most.

ONE SHOE

(in SUMMER MEMORIES, a Collection of stories, poems, and artwork published by Authors of Manitoba and Oak Island Publications)

A personal memoir about an unforgettable music festival and revelations found barefoot in the rain.

Part of a collection of original work by Manitoban authors.